W9-AEB-616

A Christmas Memory

A Christmas Memory

Richard Paul Evans

THORNDIKE PRESS
A part of Gale, a Cengage Company

Thorndike Press, part of Gale, a Cengage Company.

This book is a work of fiction. Any references to historical events, real people, or real places are used fictitiously. Other names, characters, places, and events are products of the author's imagination, and any resemblance to actual events or places or persons, living or dead, is entirely coincidental.

Thorndike Press® Large Print Basic.
The text of this Large Print edition is unabridged.
Other aspects of the book may vary from the original edition.
Set in 16 pt. Plantin.

**LIBRARY OF CONGRESS CIP DATA ON FILE.
CATALOGUING IN PUBLICATION FOR THIS BOOK
IS AVAILABLE FROM THE LIBRARY OF CONGRESS.**

ISBN-13: 979-8-8857-8387-3 (hardcover alk. paper)

Published in 2022 by arrangement with Gallery Books, a division of Simon & Schuster, Inc.

Printed in Mexico
Print Number: 1 Print Year: 2023

To Mr. Foster

AUTHOR'S N

Usually when a writer bases
experience, it is the core of t
kept intact, while the names
changed. In a way this book
of that. While the main story
of several of my childhood e
the details that remain stub
some indelibly scarred into m

It's not likely, in our day, th
would be allowed to spend ti
an older man without there
sions. Mr. Foster was, as I p
kind, older man who, to my
time for a lonely boy and als
limitless supply of Brach's cho
am grateful for that friendshi
died more than forty years ag
this book to his memory.

Prologue

As I grow older, I find that there are memories that my heart has sheltered, like an oyster around a pearl. It's an apt metaphor, I think, as the oyster forms a pearl not to create something of beauty but to protect itself from pain. But beautiful the pearl is all the same. So are my memories. I'm old enough now to realize that the most meaningful experiences of my life aren't always the ones I would have chosen to go through or would get back in line for.

One of those memories I hold particularly close. A Christmas memory of Mr. Foster. It's one I've never shared with the world. I don't know why, but in my mind, the memory still comes to me in black-and-white, like television was back then.

Caged memories do not sit well, and with each passing year, this one gnaws at me more and more to get out. Maybe that's why now, at my age, I share the story I've hidden for so long, baring my soul in ink. What you do with it, whether you find hope or pain, is up to you. Do with it as you will.

erself. But, inevitably, the day came that ny brother shipped off for Vietnam. We weren't happy to learn that he'd been assigned to the First Cavalry Division, one of the most decorated and bloodiest fighting units of the US military. The change of mood in our home was palpable. On top of the fear, there was a growing tension between my parents. My mother began voicing her disapproval with the war, though usually passively, by sharing negative headlines from the day, which there never seemed to be a dearth of.

The letters from my brother came less frequently, and, when they did, carried a new tone — a faux hopefulness as fake as a tin Rolex. The change permeated our home. Whenever a letter would come, my mother would carry it with her the whole day, occasionally reading or rereading from it. Sometimes she would read to me from his letters. Mark was always writing from places with names my mother couldn't pronounce, towns like Bien Hoa and Khe Sanh.

Even more than what they said, I remembered the way the letters looked — the red-and-blue-bordered airmail envelope was usually smudged with dirt, which made it seem like he'd sent us a piece of the country, war and all. The letters were often stained

CHAPTER 1

It was the summer of 1967. It felt to me like the world was on fire. Maybe it always has been. The Vietnam War was in full blaze. China was in the throes of a cultural revolution. America was in one of its own. Just two years earlier, the Watts neighborhood of Los Angeles exploded in a race riot just twenty miles from my home in Pasadena, and there were American soldiers in American streets. The riot was put down, but the rage continued to grow. More than a hundred riots broke out across the country that year, resulting in millions of dollars of damage, and almost a hundred deaths.

That death toll was nothing compared to the rising body count abroad. That year, the United States suffered its greatest number of casualties so far in Vietnam. In response to the rising loss of lives, the powers that be doubled down and called more boys to action — more kindling to add to that bonfire.

To me, an awkward boy of eight with Tourette's syndrome, the fear was spread thick by grim newscasters and newspaper ink. The war had special relevancy to my family. My older brother Mark — my only sibling — was somewhere in the jungles of that godawful place.

There was a sizable age gap between my brother and me, more than a decade. I don't know how that came about. In my early teens — after I learned how the whole baby-making process worked — I figured I might have just been an accident, though my mother denied it when I asked her about it. "We always wanted you," she said, which didn't really answer my question and, during some of those years, didn't even feel quite true.

I suppose my story really started before that. I was seven years old when my brother left for basic training in Fort Polk, Louisiana. It was two weeks before Thanksgiving, but we felt anything but grateful. My mother lit candles around the house and kept playing a vinyl record of "I'll Be Home for Christmas" as she dabbed her eyes with the handkerchief that always seemed to be in her hand.

My brother, Mark, was quiet and easygoing. A peacemaker. He was a good brother

and would sometimes take me to b
games when my father wasn't around,
was too often the case. He read a lo
shared with me his love for books, thou
didn't sink in for me until later in life.

The night before my brother left
service, I walked into his bedroom wrapp
in a blanket and with tears streaming dow
my cheeks. I wanted to tell him that I didn
want him to go, but I couldn't get it out. He sat down on his bed next to me and put his arm around me. "What's the matter, pal?" he asked, as if he didn't know. Finally, I got out, "What if you don't come back?"

He pulled my head into his chest. "I'll be back. I promise." He held me for a couple of minutes, then kissed the top of my head. "Now go to bed. I still need to pack."

I remember that night, lying under my blanket crying. I wanted to believe him. I wanted to believe that just his saying so was enough to control destiny. But, in reality, it's like people telling people to fly safe when they get on a plane, knowing there is absolutely nothing they can do to make that happen. Sometimes we just don't hold the controls.

The next few months passed in a sort of limbo. "At least he's still in the States," my mother would say to us, mostly to comfort with splattered drops, sweat or tears, I don't know.

The days crawled and the months flew. Like most of the war's conscripted, Mark was indentured for a one-year tour of duty. With just three more months of duty, his letters felt hopeful again. He began writing about the future and things he looked forward to, like my mom's cooking. He asked about some of the girls he used to know. He promised to be home for Christmas. He kept his promise. Just not the way we hoped.

That was the day when the reality of that conflict reached our world — when the war's suffering was not just borne by other people's sons and brothers. That was a day I'll never forget — the day a tall, wispy-haired man in an army uniform came to our door.

Chapter 2

Thursday, August 3, 1967

It was an uncomfortably warm Los Angeles day. Our little Pasadena home, surrounded by citrus trees and palms, was usually temperate, but that day the heat was spiked by the Santa Ana winds. Our home didn't have an air conditioner and a chain of oscillating fans blew around the house with a steady buzz and whisper.

My mother was wearing a sunflower-patterned sundress that I remember with unusual clarity. I've discovered that in times of calamity our minds indiscriminately capture the mundane along with the traumatic, indelibly searing images of both into our psyches. That's why people remember exactly where they were when President Kennedy was shot or the Twin Towers fell.

It was supposed to be a good day. It was the last week of my summer vacation and that afternoon my mother and I were going

CHAPTER 3

g in our home was the same after
. I didn't start school the next week.
itine of our lives turned to chaos.
ng to the information in the enve-
brother's body would be delivered
me within a week of notification,
ss they had a lot of other bodies to
ne right then, and it took longer
. It took almost three weeks. It felt
er.

neral was simple, courtesy of the
ry, not that any of us would be
em a thank-you letter.

her had six sisters, all of whom
almost seven hundred miles away
where my mother was born and
l when they got a final date for
, all six of them crowded into an
and beige Volkswagen microbus
to California.

ral for my brother was held on

on a special date, first to a Jack in the Box drive-in to get a hamburger, then to Penney's to shop for school clothes. My mother was in her bedroom gussying herself up and I was sitting at the kitchen table drawing pictures of robots (I was obsessed with them) when the doorbell rang. I got up and answered it.

A man stood a few feet from the door. In spite of the warmth of the day, he wore a tie and jacket. He was gaunt, with a protruding jaw and round granny spectacles securely perched on his bulbous nose. The jacket he wore hung from his shoulders like it would from a department store coatrack. Parked in front of our house was a car with a gold US Army star decal on its door.

"Hello, young man. Is your mother or father home?"

"Yes, sir," I said.

My mother came out of her room. "Who is it, Ricky?" she asked brightly.

"It's a man."

"A salesman?"

My mother walked toward me with her head cocked to one side as she fastened an earring. I remember her smile vanishing when she saw the man. She looked past him to his vehicle, then froze.

His voice came sincere but rehearsed.

"Mrs. Evans, I'm sorry to have to inform you —"

That's all he could get out before my mother started screaming. "No! No! No!" I had never seen my mother in hysterics before and it frightened me. "Get out of here! Leave our house! Leave. Right now!" She swatted at him like he was a fly.

The man stood there uneasily.

Why isn't he leaving? I thought.

"I'm very sorry," he repeated. He looked down at me. "Son, is your father home?"

I shook my head, still not understanding what was going on. My father was never home during the day, often not even on weekends. My father was a midlevel administrator for a chain of convalescent homes (as they called them back then) and he spent his days driving between the company's different facilities, from Bakersville to San Bernardino. He was gone a lot, which is why it was usually just my mother and me.

The man asked if we had a pastor or a family member he could call for us, but my mother just kept shouting at him to leave. Finally, he confessed his sorrow again, then dismissed himself, leaving an envelope in my mother's hands.

My mother shut the door and, leaning

against it, collapsed to t
almost a full hour before I
she was crying.

Monday, August 21, at the church in Monrovia that we sometimes attended.

There weren't a whole lot of people there, mostly friends of my brother, a few neighbors, and my mother's friends from the PTA. Outside of my visiting aunts, we had no other family.

People acted like they didn't know how to act. There was an open microphone, which mostly remained unused. One older man wearing a World War II veteran cap got up and spoke about how my brother had died a hero, defending America and the cause of freedom. He meant well, I suppose, but somehow the words felt strange to me. Vietnam was such a small country and so far away; I wasn't sure how it could threaten our country or our freedoms. I had felt much more afraid during the riots at home a couple of years before. But I didn't understand the world anyway and left the reasoning to smarter or, at least, older people.

One thing I did know was that my brother didn't believe in the war and didn't want to go. It was a point of contention in our family, one my mother was quietly stuck in the middle of. My father, who had never served in the military, told my brother that he would be ashamed of him if he didn't serve his country. In this way my family fought our own battle over the war.

Maybe it was familial or cultural pressure but, in the end, like thousands of others, my brother went. Back then people, for the most part, still implicitly trusted their country and the men who governed it. That decade was the time when the veneer started to peel from that trust.

The aunts stayed for a couple of days after the funeral, helping with meals and dishes and such, clucking and scratching about and doing their best to distract my mother from the reason they were there. One day they went to the beach, which was a first for all of them. They went in their Utah clothes and shoes and walked on the sand with as much wonder as the astronauts on their first moonwalk.

The next day, they piled into the Volkswagen bus and drove back home to Utah, their absence magnifying the vacuum of our new world.

After that, my father was around home a lot more, but, in a way, he was just as absent as before. He wasn't the same. He kept to himself and lost his temper at the slightest things. Six weeks after the funeral, my father lost his job, which created a whole new set of challenges — money problems and my parents' constant fighting. It felt like everything in my life was spiraling out of control, and I wasn't wrong. I didn't know it at the time, but my parents had decided to separate.

This was the same time that my Tourette's syndrome first manifested. My first tic was a shrug. Not much was known about Tourette's back then, and my mother just told me to stop doing it. I tried to obey, but the urge just kept coming. It was like an itch that needed to be scratched. It was just one of more than twenty different tics I would have throughout my life.

My aunts, aware of my father's unemployment and our deteriorating financial situation, offered us a place to live for free: the old house in Utah that had been left abandoned after my grandmother's death.

I never really knew my maternal grandparents. My grandfather had died before I was born, and I only really remembered being in Utah once, back when I was five. I have only hazy snapshots of memories of my grandmother — a corpulent, kind woman, smiling as she handed me a hot sugar cookie from a tray. I liked her. I knew my mother liked her, since they spoke nearly every day on the telephone. Unfortunately, life didn't afford my mother the chance to see her often, since we only had one car and it was too expensive to fly back then.

My mother was planning a trip to visit her mother for her sixty-fifth birthday when, four days before our departure, my grandmother unexpectedly died of heart failure.

Another snapshot: my mother standing over an ironing board in the kitchen, crying. I asked her why she was crying. She said her mother had gone to heaven. I asked her if heaven was a bad place. She said, "No. It's a good place." Puzzled, I asked, "Then why are you crying?" She never answered me.

My father, mother, and I drove to Utah for the funeral, then drove back the next day. That was the last time we went back to Utah. At least, until we moved there for good.

Chapter 4

Saturday, September 9

The FOR SALE sign went up in our front yard on a Saturday afternoon. I was sitting at a card table selling lemonade for five cents a Dixie cup. The sign wasn't up very long. California was booming back then, and we sold our home in just five days.

The next Saturday we had a garage sale, and my parents sold off pretty much everything they could, including all my old toys and bedroom furniture. What we didn't sell my parents left in front of the house with a sign that read FREE.

We rented a small U-Haul trailer, which my father hitched to the back of his olive-green Buick Riviera, then, with him in his car and my mother and me in our overfilled station wagon, we left our home in California.

We started out early in the afternoon, stopped briefly in Barstow, where we got a hamburger and 7 Up for dinner, then drove on, stopping for the night in Las Vegas — the halfway point to Utah.

It was a long and silent drive. I drew pictures on a notepad while my mother just followed the trailer in front of us. Every now and then I would hear a sniffle and I would look up to see her wipe her cheek.

We stayed in Las Vegas in a dodgy hotel that advertised rooms for nineteen dollars a night. The room had two twin beds. I slept in one with my mother. I didn't think it odd that my parents didn't sleep together, as the beds were small. I still didn't know they were planning on separating.

The room stank of tobacco and other unpleasant odors. That night there was a lot of noise in the hotel's parking lot. At one point my father got up and looked out the curtains, checked the chain on the door, then got back in bed.

We got up the next morning with the sun. Vegas was different back then — not the Disneyesque attraction it is today. It looked as hard as the people it drew and the casinos offered cheap meals to lure gamblers into smoky rooms that were gauchely decorated with metallic foil wallpaper and velvet wall hangings as subtle as an Elvis costume.

Just a half block down the street from our

hotel, one of the casinos offered coffee and a three-egg, hash brown, and flapjack breakfast for just eighty-nine cents. That's where we went.

A busty, frowning woman in an orange waitress uniform grabbed some menus and seated us at a table near the middle of the space. We were the only traditional-looking family in the dining room. The place was filled with truckers and salesmen and old people with cigarettes clenched between their teeth and a lever in one hand as they feverishly fed coins into slot machines with the other. Every now and then the room would ring with a siren or bell and the clanging sound of coins on tin.

"One-armed bandits," my father called the slot machines.

To me, the people seated at the machines looked lifeless, like flesh-painted statues, their eyes dull as lizards, registering no emotion even when they won. Even as a kid, I could tell the slot machines robbed them of more than just money.

We ate our breakfast, then filled the cars with gas and started off again. After an hour the desert landscape changed from flat to mountainous as we passed through the northwest corner of Arizona into the Virgin River Gorge, some of the most spectacular scenery in America. It was also listed as the most dangerous stretch of highway in America — the mountains and rock canyon walls rising hundreds of feet above the narrow byway.

"You're going to love Utah," my mother said, abruptly breaking the silence. "I have such fond memories. The people are all so nice. And having four seasons is such a treat. It's especially pretty in autumn when the leaves turn."

"Isn't it autumn now?" I asked.

"Yes. When we get to the valley, the mountains will look like a big, beautiful quilt. Maybe this weekend we'll take a drive through the canyons to gather leaves."

It seemed like a strange idea to me. In California my father and I raked leaves just to put them in the garbage can. "What do we do with the leaves?"

"We gather them."

For the next ten minutes my mother spoke glowingly of her childhood and her idyllic memories. They were clearly the halcyon days of her life.

About a half hour into the canyon pass our trailer got a flat tire and pieces of rubber flipped up into the air. It was likely the worst possible place in the world to get a flat tire, so I wasn't surprised it happened.

Street. We drove east up 3900 South,
few small retail businesses, until we
o a two-pump gas station named the
Depot and turned right. There was a
nd sign at the mouth of the road and
ner drove to the end of the street past
box-shaped, vinyl-sided homes with
worn aluminum awnings.

were no sidewalks or streetlamps,
holes and clumps of unkempt pyra-
bushes and oiled telephone poles,
of them strung together with sag-
etal power lines — a depressing
te for the cloistered palm trees of
ia.

andmother's house was at the end
reet, where the asphalt gave way to
-rock gravel road, leading into a
ndeveloped tract of land. Even
d been to my grandparents' house
had no recollection of it. The house
ler than our home in California,
the many cobbled-on additions
out of it. What paint remained on
was faded olive green, though
e places where patches of the
rker green, shielded from the sun
ing or overhang, were still visible.
er pulled the trailer a little past
ay, then stopped. He got out of

It was a metaphor of what our life was like these days.

My dad sidled his car and trailer as close to the cement wall barrier as he could, turned on his warning flashers, and got out as my mother pulled up behind him. He walked to my mom's open window and said, "Turn on your flashers and don't get out," though I doubt that the thought of getting out of our car in this kill zone had crossed either of our minds.

I leaned against the door and looked out the window. To my astonishment there was a mountain goat standing hundreds of feet up on the side of the sheer rock wall. I wondered how it had gotten itself in such a predicament and how it was going to get down.

"There's a goat," I said to my mother.

She leaned over to look out my window. "Isn't that something?"

"How's he going to get down?" I asked.

"I don't know. Sometimes we get ourselves in predicaments, don't we," she said. "Would you like some licorice?"

My mother loved black licorice and usually had a bag of it in her purse. That and those Choward's Violet mints. I wasn't a big fan of licorice, at least not the black stuff, but we didn't get many treats around our house so I would never turn candy down.

"Yes. Thank you."

It took my father just fifteen minutes to fix the tire and get us back on the road. The goat was still on the perch as we drove off.

An hour later we passed a tall blue sign that read:

UTAH WELCOMES YOU

The weather was still warm in Utah. In fact, it seemed even warmer than Pasadena, which wasn't at all what I had expected. My mother had told me so many stories about walking to school in three feet of snow (all parents do) that I imagined the Utah ground perpetually covered beneath a knee-high blanket of snow. I didn't know that there was such a significant elevation and climate change between the mountainous regions of the Wasatch Front and the southernmost city of Saint George, Utah, which was closer in elevation and climate to Palm Springs, California.

Saint George has an interesting history. About a century earlier, after putting down stakes in the territory, the Mormon pioneer leader Brigham Young sent devotees south to create their own version of "Dixieland," planting fields of cotton and sorghum. In

his car and walked back to us. My mother rolled down her window.

"Home sweet home," he said sardonically.

My mother didn't say anything.

"I'm going to park the trailer in the driveway. Back up a little."

My father reversed his car until the trailer began to jackknife in the direction of the house. After the trailer had crossed the front of the driveway, he pulled forward to even out his approach, then slowly backed the trailer down the gravel driveway, his tires spitting pebbles as he corrected, then corrected again. He stopped when the back of the trailer was adjacent to the walkway that led to the front door.

My mother parked the station wagon in front of the house parallel to an irrigation ditch — a great, weed-filled furrow half filled with a fast-moving stream of water that ran the length of the road.

"Can you get out?" my mother asked.

I looked out the window. "Yeah."

"Don't fall in the ditch."

"I won't."

We got out of the car about the same time my father did. The weather was much cooler than it was in Saint George, probably around the low sixties.

I looked at the house with apprehension. I

could imagine the whole thing collapsing on us in the night while we slept.

A dusty row of narrow pines separated our driveway from our next-door neighbor's yard, which, unlike those of the other homes on the street, was reasonably well kept.

The house directly across the street from us looked like a flea market. It had a toilet in the front yard next to a rusted water heater. A tow truck was parked in the driveway.

After getting out, my father leaned against his car to stretch his legs. "How long has it been?" he asked my mother.

"A moment," she said. This was about the extent of my parents' conversations of late.

The front porch stretched across half of the home's facade and looked as if it had been tacked on to the house as an afterthought, which it no doubt was. It was built from two-by-fours and sheets of plywood and enclosed with rusted metal screens. The porch door was held shut with a long, rusted spring about half a foot long and secured with a small steel hook.

My father unlatched the door and opened it, stepping in cautiously, as if he expected to encounter something or fall through a rotted floor. The plank floor creaked noisily as we followed him inside.

There was a cardboard box on the floor near the door with a note on it.

Welcome home, June

My father's and my name were noticeably absent.

"My sisters left us a housewarming gift," my mother said. "That was sweet of them."

"A care package from the old birds," my father said.

I didn't think my father liked my aunts, since he'd left the house the moment they arrived in California. I think it was mutual. They never forgave him for taking their sister out of Utah.

My mother squatted down to forage through the box. It was filled with an eclectic mix of things, mostly foodstuffs — bread, flour, a tub of margarine, a carton of milk, and a bag of homemade chocolate chip cookies. There were a few other boxes and things, like Pine-Sol spray and light bulbs.

My father tried the brass doorknob. "It's locked."

"They left a key," my mother said. "It should be in here." My mother tipped up a terra-cotta flowerpot that was partially filled with potting soil and retrieved a single key from beneath. "We kept it here when I was a child," she said. "Some things never change."

"Your sisters haven't," my father said.

My mother unlocked the door and opened it, then stepped inside. If there was any special emotion attached to my mother's return home, she didn't show it.

The home felt colder inside than it was outside. The front room, or what I could discern of it in the dim light, was still occupied by my grandmother's old things, floor lamps, hung pictures, and knick-knacks.

What struck me most, besides the room's dampness and shuttered darkness, was the smell. The home had a dank pungency. I know now that it was mildew, but back then I just thought it was the way old things smelled.

The place *was* old. It looked to me like it was old when they built it, back before there were building codes and inspections and people just threw things up based on what they could find or afford at the moment. Much of the home's wiring was exposed. There was wallpaper, faded florals of vertically lined daffodils.

"It smells," I said.

My father grinned. "Don't sniff a gift

house in the mouth." He flipped a light switch up and down, but nothing happened.

"Geniel said the power was still on," my mother said.

"The lightbulbs are probably burned out." My father rooted through the box that my aunts had left and brought out a box of lightbulbs.

"Looks like the old birds saved me a trip to the hardware store."

"Stop calling them that," my mother said. "They're not old."

"Only in spirit," he said.

He took the box into the next room, the dining area, and set it on the table. My mother and I followed him in.

The room was noticeably brighter than the front room, with two large windows veiled behind sheer pink and lilac curtains. There was a wrought-iron wood-burning stove in the corner of the room and an oblong dining table in the middle — big enough to fit a family of nine. My mother opened the curtains, brightening the room still more.

The dining room was the heart of the home, with three main arteries: one leading to the front room, one to the hall corridor and bedrooms, and the third into the kitchen.

I followed my mother into the kitchen. It had red Formica countertops with speckles of black and gold glitter and rimmed with a ridged aluminum casing. A large porcelain sink was inset beneath the room's only window. Oak-veneered cabinets hung from the back wall.

The main appliances in the room were an old gas stove and a porcelain-white Coldspot refrigerator. The refrigerator was large and bulbous, like the hood of a 1950s Cadillac. The door was accented by a V-shaped emblem with the name Coldspot spelled out in an art deco script.

My mother opened the refrigerator.

"The fridge works. The light is burned out."

"No surprise there," my father said from another room. "They must have left everything on after your mother died."

"How do you leave a fridge light on?" she said defensively. She suddenly winced. "Oh. Someone left milk in here. It must be a year old."

"Check it for a pulse," my father said.

"Ha, ha," my mother replied. She poured the curdled milk down the sink.

The kitchen had a back door that led out to the pantry — another cobbled-on room, similar to the porch at the front of the house. My mother walked out to explore the space.

"There's some bottled fruit," she said. "There's probably a lot more of it in the cellar."

"How old is it?" my father asked from the other room.

"I don't know. Mom wrote the dates on the lids." She pulled out a jar and dusted off the brassy top. "Six years old."

"Is any of it still good?"

"Mom always said her food storage would outlast her. I guess she was right."

Along the pantry's outer wall were wooden crates stacked waist-high with dusty Kerr bottles. The outsides of the crates were scrawled with the boxes' contents: peaches, beets, or blueberries. There were also large rectangular cans with labels that read RED WINTER WHEAT.

My mother asked, "Are you hungry?"

I didn't answer. It seemed that I was always hungry, but I was afraid she was thinking of feeding me something from those dusty bottles. Before I could answer, she handed me a jar of peaches.

"You can have some of these. Wash the bottle off in the sink. There should be some forks in one of the drawers. After we unpack, I'll make pancakes."

I took the bottle of fruit back into the kitchen and began looking through the drawers for utensils. There were things still in them, many of which looked like medieval torture devices — like a wood-handled eggbeater, an egg separator, and an apple corer-peeler machine.

I washed the glass jar, which turned the sink brown with mud, then pried off the jar's lid and speared a ripe peach half. It was a little rubbery, but it tasted better than I expected.

"How are they?" my mother asked, walking back into the kitchen.

"They're okay. When I'm done can I explore the yard?"

"Don't run off just yet. We still need to unpack the car."

"Yes, ma'am. Where is my room?"

"Just down the hall, past the bathroom."

I finished the jar of peaches, then walked down to my new bedroom, stopping first to use the bathroom. The bathroom was long and narrow, with an old tub, the kind that had claws, and a curtain that could be pulled around it.

The tub was just inches from an old porcelain toilet that had a wooden seat and a tank near the ceiling with pipes running down to the bowl. After finishing my business, I flushed the toilet by pulling a wooden knob connected to a chain. The thing looked like it belonged in a museum, but it worked, so there was that.

I walked to my bedroom. As I opened the door I could hear the scurrying of rodents. I looked around, then cautiously stepped inside. There were mice droppings all over the floor.

When my mother was a child, this was her bedroom, which she shared with five of her sisters. It was walled with wood paneling and had two windows, which for curtains used old, yellow-stained bedsheets hung over wooden dowels.

The home's design was labyrinthian, and my bedroom was also a corridor, as it led to another smaller room and then an even smaller one after that.

The second room had been used for storage and contained an ancient black upright piano with boxes stacked all around it. The last room was empty except for an old bed frame, mouse poop, and rodent bones.

My father shouted for me. I walked back out to the front yard, where my father was standing next to the open trailer. There were boxes scattered around the lawn.

"Just start carrying these into the house," he said, lifting a box.

My father and I stacked things on one end of the front room, while my mother opened the boxes, then distributed their contents to their final destination.

After we had brought everything inside, my mother handed me some sheets. "Put these on your bed. I'll make it later."

"Where are you and Dad sleeping?"

"The first room from the dining room," she said. "But tonight, you and I will sleep in there. Dad will sleep in your bed."

"I can sleep in my own bed."

"It's just for tonight. You can go outside and play while I make dinner."

I set the folded sheets on my bed, then went outside. My grandparents had owned at least five acres of property, land they purchased when this part of the valley was still considered the boondocks. Since then, the city had grown up around their home.

At the end of the gravel driveway there was a work-shed garage painted the same color as the house. It was large, a few feet taller than the house.

If the house was mouse infested, the garage was overrun. It was Mouseville. As I walked inside, the place crawled around me.

My grandfather had been a pharmacist by trade. He had spent most of his life working at the Woolworth pharmacy, but, like most men of his time, he was also a tinkerer. He had a workspace filled with old, rusted tools, none of which were electric; a hand drill, planers and hammers and saws — sharp things that would elicit a parent's worry today, but not so much back then. There were wonderful implements everywhere; gears and pulleys and hooks and cables, treasures for an eight-year-old boy.

Connected to the old shed was a greenhouse. It was wood-framed and still retained about half of its glass; the rest was broken out, whether by nature or vandals I didn't know. There were still planting trays and empty pots and old faded packages of plant seeds.

Other than cobwebs, there was nothing growing in the space, though it wasn't hard to imagine that it had once been someplace bright and alive. I remember my mother telling me that her father had a green thumb, which I had taken literally until I was about eight.

I walked out into the backyard as grasshoppers hopped up around me from the overgrown weeds like popcorn from a hot skillet. There was a small orchard of fruit trees. In California we had an orange tree, a lemon tree, and an avocado tree. Here there were more than a dozen trees — green and red apples, pears, peaches, sweet cherries, plums, and one black walnut.

I climbed up into the fork of a pear tree and picked a golden-spotted pear, then sat there and ate. The fruit was deliciously ripe, and juice ran down my jaw and chin. I had found something good here. I finished the pear, then continued my exploration.

On the south side of our yard, separating our home from the vacant field, was a clear, slow-moving creek. It was about a dozen feet wide and deep enough that I couldn't see the bottom.

I walked along the bank of the creek until the weeds came up to my waist, then headed farther back in the field until I came to where I found the wooden post end of a barbed-wire fence. There were faded and rusty NO TRESPASSING signs wired to the fence. I figured this was the end of our property, so I headed back toward the house.

Along the way I found the skull and spine of an animal, small for a dog but with a snout narrower than a cat's. It looked old and desiccated and probably had been there for a long time. I wondered if there might be other wild animal bones back there as well. Maybe even a dinosaur fossil or two.

In the back of the yard was a sturdy old

henhouse built of cinder block with a slanted tin roof. There were no hens inside, only the faint whisp of sulfur, chicken poop, and damp rotted hay.

This would make a good fort, I thought. I was pretty sure that those concrete walls could stop bullets. Who would attack the house with guns was beyond me, but in an eight-year-old boy's mind there was never a lack of villains.

I was checking the individual hen nest boxes for old eggs when I heard my mother calling, so I continued back to the house.

When I walked inside it was just my mother sitting at the table. She looked upset, even more than usual. I wondered if my parents had been fighting again.

My mother had made blueberry pancakes, boiling down the juice from the jarred berries into a syrup. There was a stack of pancakes on a plate next to a glass of milk.

I sat down next to her.

"I buttered your pancakes already," she said. "I made blueberry syrup. Your favorite."

"Thank you." I poured some syrup, took a bite of pancake, then looked around. "Where's Dad?"

"He's getting ready for bed," she said softly. After a moment she pushed back a little from the table to look at me. "I need to tell you something."

I recognized the tone of her voice. It was the one that always preceded bad news. I stopped eating and looked at her.

"I'm sure you've noticed that your dad and I haven't been getting along very well lately."

I didn't want to have this conversation, but I knew it wasn't going away.

"Yeah."

"We've decided that we're going to separate for a little while."

My chest froze. *Separate* was just a code word for divorce. I had a friend in California whose parents got divorced. It wasn't good.

"You mean . . . divorce?"

"I didn't say that," she said. "Right now we just need a little space between us."

I went back to eating, but I could feel the weight of her eyes on me. My face started twitching.

"You know when you got that blister on your foot last summer?"

I couldn't conceive what that could possibly have to do with what we were talking about.

"The first thing you did was take your shoe off, right? So it wouldn't keep irritating the sore. That's what this is like. We both have a lot of pain right now. We all do since Mark . . ." She stopped. Her eyes welled up. "Anyway, I don't think things will get any better unless we take the shoe off. Does that make sense?"

Nothing in my life made sense. I ate for a moment in silence, then looked back up at her.

"Am I going back to California?"

"No one's going back to California. Your dad's staying in Utah. He has an old friend here whom he's going to move in with for a little while, while we figure things out. So you'll still see him every week."

"He's leaving us?"

She suddenly got emotional. "I'm sorry." She got up and took her plate into the kitchen.

I just sat there alone. I wasn't hungry anymore. I don't know why I was surprised. They had been headed down this road since Mark died. There was nothing left for our family to lose. Or so I thought.

Chapter 5

I woke the next morning to the smell of coffee and low voices in the kitchen. I had slept in the queen-sized bed with my mother, and she was gone when I woke.

I walked out to the dining room to find my mother and father talking. My mother was wearing a robe but my father was fully dressed, wearing a suit and tie. At my entrance, my mother's brow furrowed and she stopped talking.

My father turned to me. "Hey, sport. How'd you sleep?"

"Okay."

"At least the rats didn't eat you."

My mother shook her head, then walked into the kitchen. After she was gone my father turned back to me. "So, your mother told me she talked to you . . . about us . . ." He hesitated, maybe hoping that I would fill in the blank so he wouldn't have to say it. I didn't. Finally he breathed out slowly. ". . .

splitting up."

"She said you're separating."

He nodded, his eyes glued on me, looking for my reaction. "That's right. Are you okay?"

I don't know what he expected me to say. Nothing was *okay.* My brother was dead, our house gone, now my parents were separating. Every part of my life was being torn apart. What part of me was supposed to be okay?

"It doesn't matter." I don't know why I said that. It was exactly opposite to the way I felt.

My father just frowned. "So, anyway. I'm leaving now. I'm staying with a friend for a while. But I'm not leaving your life."

I wasn't sure what he meant by that last sentence. "But you just said you were leaving."

"There will be changes." He was quiet again, then said, "I'll be back in a few days to pick up some things. Maybe I could take you to McDonald's for a burger. How does that sound?"

I shrugged.

"I know it's hard. It's hard on all of us." He ran his hand through my hair. "Take care of your mother." He stood.

"Dad?"

"Yeah?"

"Are you ever coming back for good?"

The question hung in the air. After a minute he said, "We'll see." He glanced over at my mother, who had stepped back into the room, then he picked up the two suitcases near the door and walked out. I ran out to the backyard so no one could see me crying.

CHAPTER 6

The north side of our backyard, the side opposite the creek, was the one region of the property I had yet to explore. It was lined with a wood-slat fence that, unlike everything else around the property, had been reasonably well maintained.

Our neighbor on that side, whom I had yet to see, had a backyard full of trees and a sizable berry patch. A spray of berries fell over the fence onto our side, which, in my book, meant they were ours. I didn't know what kind of berries they were, but they looked good. I walked over and picked some. I popped a berry into my mouth; it was both sweet and bitter. *Not as good as a raspberry,* I thought. I looked through a slat in the fence to see where this fruit had come from.

My neighbor's berry patch contained blueberries, blackberries, elderberries, Goji berries, and a long hedge of raspberries.

Whoever lived there clearly put work into the cultivation of the fruit. There was only one fruit tree — an apricot tree.

I was blinking and twitching from my Tourette's, something I did when I was upset or anxious. Then my heart just burst. I leaned against the fence and sobbed so hard that I had trouble catching my breath. I just wanted to wake from this nightmare. I felt scared and alone.

I had been crying for several minutes when my sobs were interrupted by the friendly yelp of a dog. I looked down to see the thin snout of a dog protruding between the narrow gap between the ground and the fence. He barked playfully, trying to get through the fence to me.

"Hey, boy," I said. I put my hand up to his nose and he began frantically licking me.

"You're friendly," I said. "Good boy."

The dog's licks had a therapeutic effect on my pain. I had always wanted a dog. I had asked for one for my sixth birthday — then every birthday and Christmas since then — but my mother just said it would mean she would have to take care of it, so I ended up with a goldfish instead. Then, when that didn't stop my begging, my parents gave me a red-eared slider box turtle — the kind with a bright red streak on its head and a yellow underbelly. Turtles were common in California before they were determined to carry a contagious disease and banned from pet stores. Still, reptiles aren't really something you can bond with. I wasn't even sad when it ran away, which seems ironic for something that can't really climb and is infamous for moving so slowly.

"What's your name, boy? Do you have a name?"

I put my eye up to the slat in the fence so I could see the dog. He was smallish, maybe ten pounds, with curly black-and-white fur markings like a Holstein cow. He had a black patch of fur over one eye and one of his ears was flopped back. His tail was wagging like a car's windshield wipers in a downpour.

"You're a handsome dog," I said. When I was younger my mother affectionately called me Beau Brummell to say I looked handsome. I had no idea who that was, but it always made me happy. "I'll call you Beau," I said.

I decided he liked the name because he wouldn't stop licking me. "Good Beau."

I almost forgot about how bad the morning had been. At least I had found a friend in this awful place.

Chapter 7

When I was six years old, my brother took me to Disneyland. It was a weekday and there weren't a lot of people there. As the park was closing, we ran into the Pirates of the Caribbean attraction for one last ride. There was no one else in line, so, halfway through the ride the workers shut it down with us still on it. We sat there for fifteen minutes listening to the "Yo Ho" song and yelling for help. That's what my life felt like right now.

With the exception of my new furry friend, things grew increasingly worse. With my father gone, my mother's emotional state seemed to decline. She complained of having a lot of migraines, which she described as a headache multiplied by a hundred. She spent a lot of time in bed in her darkened bedroom. In fact, it seemed she was always there.

Every now and then one of my aunts

would come by to check on my moth
Sometimes they brought their husbands t
all quiet men who followed their wi
around like shadows and never spoke to
Their visits were never pleasant. They wo
indignantly huff about the house, pick
up things and doing the dishes and w
ing, always sure to let me know what a s
man my father was. Then, before leav
they would scold me with, "You nee
take better care of your mother."

Sadly, I believed them, even thou
wasn't sure how I was supposed to do
I didn't know how messed up that
was. Young children aren't supposed to
care of their parents.

I should have been in school, but n
seemed to worry about that — least
me. It's always scary to step into
community, but something about th
just didn't feel right. I told myself t
all our family problems, my mother
waiting until school came aroun
Like the circus. Or Halley's comet

Every morning I went out to se
really wanted to let Beau out o
but I figured I'd probably get in t
lose my only friend, or end up
dognapping. My imagination
that way.

Still, I wanted to see more of the dog, so I got one of the old saws from the garage and cut out a bottom slat in the fence so Beau could stick his whole head all the way through.

It wasn't easy cutting the fence, not just because the saw was rusty and dull but mostly because Beau wouldn't leave me alone as I tried to do it, sticking his nose around the blade. I eventually had to come back at night when he was in his house to finish cutting the board.

I always kept an eye out for other kids my age, hoping to strike up a friendship, but here weren't many around me. There was ne family on our street with at least six hildren, five of whom were girls, but they ever left their chain-link-fenced yard and l went inside whenever I walked past their ome. They were peculiar in other ways. hey dressed old-fashioned, like the people 1 *Little House on the Prairie.* The girls wore ng dresses, sometimes with pants beneath em, which I could see at their ankles, and eir hair was thickly braided like rope. It uldn't be until I was older that I realized y were polygamist children, a subculture d never encountered in California.

Chapter 8

It was later that week that I got my first glimpse of my neighbor next door. I was at the fence playing with Beau when I heard the man call for his dog. His voice was low and gruff. I couldn't tell what he was calling Beau. It was something like "Collin" or "Call 'em." Whatever it was, Beau just kept licking me.

The man kept coming closer, talking to his dog. "What did you find, boy? What have you got there?"

I looked through the slats at the approaching man. He was Black, which in Utah back then was almost as rare as a palm tree. He was a little taller than my father, broader, not fat but with an ironic pouch of a stomach. He was elderly and had gray hair and a gray beard. He walked slowly, leaning against a cane. I was afraid that he would see what I'd done to his fence, so I said good-bye to Beau, then ran back to my house.

That night my mother came out of her room to make dinner.

"I saw the man next door," I said.

My mother nodded. "That's Mr. Foster. He's lived here a long time. He moved in when I was a little girl."

"You know him?"

"Not well," she said. "He keeps to himself, mostly."

"He's Black."

"Yes, he is."

"There aren't many Black people in Utah," I said.

"Not as many as there were in California."

That's all she said. I don't think my mother was comfortable around Black people. I remember, in Pasadena, when a Black man came to our door selling Tupperware. I was maybe five at the time and was standing at her side. I could sense both of their discomfort.

The man was overly polite. "Yes, ma'am. Sorry to bother you, ma'am. I'm here with some fine kitchen containers that will make your life easier."

My mother said, "No, thank you," and shut the door. My mother was raised in Utah and, other than her neighbor, had only met one Black man her entire life. Utah's as

, then start out on a new adventure. times I would come in at lunchtime to hat my mother had made me a tuna nut butter sandwich and left it on the n counter before going back to her but usually I would pick fruit for and, sometimes, gather walnuts, would crack with an old hammer I n the shed.

we were fairly poor, but that wasn't concern to me since we didn't seem se off than anyone else around us. ways, unless you're hungry, poverty y a matter of comparison. My idn't get out to go shopping much, te a lot of the canned food from pantry. That and Campbell's Bean n soup. I ate a lot of that.

my mother asked me to walk he Milk Depot at the end of our et a bottle of milk. When I got ticed there were crates outside empty soda and milk bottles. A them read 5¢ DEPOSIT per d seen old milk bottles in the even on the way to the store I t least a half dozen soda bottles treet.

he door rang as I walked in. n old man sitting behind the

homogeneous as whole milk.

That's all she said about our neighbor. But from then on, I kept my eye out for him. I was certain that he had discovered the hole I'd cut in his fence, and it was just a matter of time before he would get mad at me. It was just something else for me to worry about.

Chapter 9

In my mother's emotional and physical condition, she didn't go out of the house for days at a time. Sometimes not even out of her bedroom. With my father gone and my mother mostly absent, I spent my days exploring the property. And I started building a robot.

Back in California, my third-grade teacher had read to us a book called *Andy Buckram's Tin Men.* The book was about a boy who built robots out of soup cans. Then, one day, a big storm came and, in a *Frankenstein*-inspired twist, lightning struck his robots and they all came to life. It was a wonderful fantasy for a lonely boy.

I conceived of other adventures. There was a long section of the creek behind our house that was so overgrown on both sides that I couldn't get to it on land. I found two old truck-tire inner tubes in the garage that still held air. I pumped them up with a bicycle

pump, then carried them o
along with some twine and
sheet of plywood. I tied
plywood, then dragged m
of the creek. I flipped it o
and jumped onto it as i
bank. I felt as brave an
Polo or Magellan.

My craft floated stea
into uncharted territor
of some zoo-worthy
beaver or muskrat, w
me trying to escape.

I never told my mo
which was probabl
had gotten in trou
ever found me. Th
back then.

I considered b
adventure, but
dognapping by t
deterrent. Still,
experience with
had a long way

Looking bac
for a young b
temporarily,
my world. I
this would b
it. I would

cerea
Some
find t
or pea
kitche
room,
lunch
which I
found i

I gues
really a
any wor
In many
is largel
mother d
and we a
the back
with Baco

One day
down to th
street to g
there, I no
filled with
sign above
bottle. I ha
garage and
had passed a
littering my s

A bell on t
There was a

counter.

"Good afternoon," he said.

"Good afternoon," I repeated. I thought he looked like an old ship skipper with a trim gray beard that ran from one side of his jaw to the other. I got a bottle of milk from the store's cooler and took it up to the man.

"One bottle of milk," he said. "That'll be fifty-two cents, plus a nickel deposit."

I set the dollar bill my mother had given me on the counter.

"Out of one George Washington, that will be forty-three cents change."

"Do you buy old bottles?" I asked.

"I refund the deposit on them," he said. "When you bring your milk bottle back, I'll give you your nickel back. Same holds true for soda bottles."

This sounded too good to be true.

"If I bring you a bottle you'll give me a nickel for it?"

"That's how it works."

"Even if I found the bottle?"

"I don't care where it comes from," he said. "A bottle's a bottle."

"Thank you," I said. I walked back to my house with the milk, then got a pillowcase from home and started walking my street looking for bottles. In the next hour I collected more than twenty bottles. I took them to the Depot.

"You're back," the man said. "Looks like you got serious about collecting bottles."

"I found them."

"Good for you," he said. "You're an entrepreneur."

"What's that?"

"A businessman."

I liked that.

"Let me help you." He lifted my bag, then started counting the bottles. "Eighteen, nineteen, twenty, twenty-one. I've got twenty-one. That sound right?"

"Yes, sir."

"That comes to one dollar and a nickel." He opened the cash register and handed me a dollar bill and a coin. I suddenly felt rich.

"Thank you," I said.

"It's a pleasure doing business with you," he said. "Come back anytime."

"How much are the peanut butter cups?"

"They are ten cents apiece."

"I'd like two of them, please."

"Two Reese's Peanut Butter Cups." He set two packages on the counter. I put them both into my front pocket.

"Shouldn't you be in school?" he asked.

The question scared me. "I haven't started

even remember.
nother did. She was up early that
ng. She made me a breakfast of
and a glass of strawberry milk.
that evening my father came home
g a bucket of Kentucky Fried
. I hadn't seen him for almost two
We also had what Utahns call
but the rest of the world calls fry
elephant ears.
of my fears, I got some pretty cool
that year — a Mickey Mouse
giant jawbreaker, a bag of Swedish
best of all, a Fort Knox toy safe
with a working combination dial.
g to need it with all the money I
g refunding bottles. Up till then
eeping my money in an old Kerr

pened my presents, my mother
t a chocolate cake. As she lit the
s, I remember feeling happy for
e in a long time, not just because
irthday, but because we were all
er. It wasn't the life we'd once
gave me hope that things might
in. At least things were on the

ow that everything was about
ain.

yet. I'm new here."

"Let's just hope the truancy officer doesn't catch you."

"What's a truancy officer?"

"He's the guy they pay to make sure kids go to school."

I didn't know if he was joking or not, but I was terrified.

"I'm just kidding with you," he said. "Can I get you anything else?"

"I'd like to have a grape soda, too." I put the money he'd given me back on the counter.

"One grape Nehi. That is also a dime, plus a nickel bottle deposit, which you will get back when you bring back the bottle. With the two peanut butter cups, that comes to thirty-five cents. Out of a dollar five, you get seventy cents back." He gave me two quarters and two dimes.

"Look at that," he said.

"What?"

"Those are mercury dimes. They're real silver."

I took a closer look at them. They looked different than other dimes I'd seen.

"Hang on to those. Those are going to be worth something."

"Thank you." I put them in my pants pocket.

"Want me to open that bottle for you?"

"Yes, sir."

There was a bottle opener mounted to the counter. He popped off the cap, which was followed by the fizz of carbonation and the cap bouncing on the tile floor. "There you go. Enjoy."

"Thank you."

I walked out of the Depot. I took a drink of my soda, then sat down on the concrete step outside the front door. I was already thinking about where I'd find my next bottles.

The work on my robot continued. It started, basically, as a small metal oil drum with a head and a claw. The head came from an old ventriloquist dummy I found in the back room in a box next to the piano. I cut the head from the body, put a stick through it, then glued it to the drum. The robot's arm, which stuck out of the middle of its body, was a simple narrow board with a hinge in the middle for an elbow. I attached a spring to the arm so it stuck straight out, which all robots on TV looked like.

My next challenge was to make a hand so it could pick things up. While I was rummaging through the garage looking for a hook, I found an old telephone magneto — a hand-cranked electrical generator that had

come from inside an old t
you would wind the han
operator. I held the gen
netic casing and twiste
one-hundred-volt shock
knocked me off my fe
been happier. Every re
some means of self-de
cal shock was almost a
I just had to figure ou
to my robot.

Autumn was windi
were falling. Back ir
see my father and
there was no talk c
just too many. It
empty the creek w
leaves would be
thought.

The untethered
time I didn't ev
with the except
day I was parti
October 11 was

Birthdays ha
bration at our
California bef
wasn't so sur
asked me wh
and the nig

would

My
mornin
waffles

Later
carryin
Chicken
weeks.
"scones"
bread or

In spite
presents
watch, a
Fish, and
coin bank
I was goin
was makin
I'd been k
jar.

After I o
brought ou
nine candle
the first tim
it was my b
back togeth
had, but it
be good aga
right track.

I didn't kn
to change ag

CHAPTER 10

Tuesday, October 17

It was the following Tuesday when I came back into the house from my morning sojourn and found my mother standing in the kitchen. She was dressed and her hair was done up.

"I've been looking for you," she said. "Where have you been?"

After all these weeks, it was a peculiar question. *Same place I always am,* I thought.

"I was out back," I said. "How come you're dressed up?" I could tell from her expression that she didn't like the question.

"I'm taking you to school. It started back up yesterday."

Her news struck me like a lightning bolt. "I don't want to go to school."

She looked surprised. "What would you do if you didn't go to school?"

I could have told her a hundred things, but I said the first thing that sounded credible. "I'm building a robot."

"A robot?"

"He's in the garage."

She seemed a little surprised. Then she said, "Well, you can still do that on the weekends. You need to go to school."

"Why?"

"Because that's what children do."

"Why?"

"So they can have a future."

"What if I don't have a future?"

"Don't be silly. Everyone has a future."

"Mark didn't."

She slapped me. My mother had never struck me before. I think it surprised her as much as it did me. My face and heart stung and my eyes watered. Adding to my pain was the shame I felt. I must have said something terrible to have provoked such a response. I was twitching like crazy.

"I'm sorry," my mother said. Her eyes welled up and she looked even more upset than I was. She put her arms around me. "I'm really sorry."

"It's okay," I said.

She breathed out heavily. "No, it's not. Please just go put on your best jeans and your red shirt. We'll go shopping for school clothes this weekend."

I went off to my room to change my

clothes. It crossed my mind that I could run away with Beau. I had more than two dollars in my bank. But where would I go? I had no idea how to walk back to California. And someone had probably moved into our house by then anyway.

Chapter 11

My heart still stung as we made the short drive to the school. At the end of our street my mother said, “You’ll walk home after school. You know our street. The Milk Depot is right there.”

“I know,” I said. I’d been there at least a dozen times on my own. I even knew Cliff, the man who owned the Milk Depot.

We turned east on Thirty-Ninth and drove just a couple of blocks, where we stopped at the intersection next to Lincoln Elementary School. Just south of the school there were two small convenience stores: a 7-Eleven and the other, a small food mart called Heller’s. (A popular saying at the school was, “Oh thank HEAVEN for 7-Eleven. So we don’t have to go to HELL-er’s.”)

It was a little after ten o’clock when we pulled into the school’s parking lot next to the bus drop-off. Through the chain-link fence I could see the children playing outside for recess.

I had seen the school a hundred times before — we drove by it almost every time we went somewhere — but I hadn't paid much attention to it. It didn't look anything like the school I had come from. Unlike my school in California, it was completely enclosed.

As we got out of our car a bell rang, announcing the end of recess. By the time we walked inside, the halls were teeming with children.

I immediately disliked the place. The school looked more like a hospital or prison than a place of learning. It even smelled old, like one of the convalescent centers my father ran. I was twitching like crazy.

My mother looked around, then said, "The office is over there."

The office wasn't hard to find. It had a large oak door with a thick cast bronze plaque that read OFFICE. My mother opened the door and we stepped inside. The space had a long laminate counter that looked like it had been mauled by a million children.

A portly woman with a massive beehive hairdo was talking to a child who, I quickly deduced, had forgotten to bring his lunch.

"You're just going to have to eat school

lunch today," she said. "I'll borrow you a ticket."

"Can I call my mom? I don't like school lunch."

"Then don't forget your lunch pail."

He took the ticket from her and walked off. The woman turned to us. "May I help you?"

"Good morning," my mother said. "We're the Evanses. This is my son, Rick. We just moved here from California. We'd like to enroll him in your school."

She furtively glanced at me. "How old is your son?"

"He turned nine last week."

"Just a moment." She went to her desk and took out a form, which she brought back to the counter. "Fill that out, please. There are pens in the can there."

While my mother filled out the form, the woman went to a file cabinet and began searching through it. After a few minutes my mother said, "I'm done."

The woman walked back to the counter and took the form. "You didn't put in your husband's name."

My mother hesitated for a moment, then just said, "Sorry." She wrote it down.

The woman took the form. "We have room in Mrs. Covey's class. That's room

109. Let me write this up, then I'll walk you to class."

The woman went back to her desk. After a moment she said, "Did your boy bring a sack lunch today, or will you be eating school lunch?"

I doubt my mother had even thought about that. "School lunch," she said.

"You can buy tickets for a month of lunch for ten dollars. You can write a check for that."

My mother took out her checkbook from her purse. "Who do I make the check out to?"

"Lincoln Elementary lunch," she said.

My mother filled out the check and gave it to the woman, who handed her a roll of yellow tickets.

"All right, let's go." She walked out from behind the counter and we followed her out into the now-empty hall. The hallway was broad, with tile walls covered with pictures drawn by students. Our footsteps echoed down the corridor. A bespectacled boy ran past us awkwardly lugging a cello case that was almost as big as he was.

"You're late, Mr. Platt," the woman said to him.

The boy turned back. "I forgot my instrument," he said.

"You'd forget your head if it wasn't screwed on," she shouted at the fleeing boy.

We stopped in front of a classroom door and the office woman opened it. The first person I saw was a stout, gray-haired woman standing at the front of the class, gesticulating as if she were preaching a sermon. When she saw us she stopped abruptly, looking annoyed by our intrusion. At first glance I thought Mrs. Covey looked like Mrs. Claus without the smile.

The kids all looked at me like I was a new inmate walking into prison. I had to force myself not to tic.

"Mrs. Covey," our escort said. "You have a new student."

The woman handed her a paper. Mrs. Covey looked over the paper, then me, then said gruffly, "Take that empty desk right there."

"Yes, ma'am." I glanced back at my mom but she was already moving toward the door. As I walked to the desk someone said, "Hey, Noah. Where's the flood?" A few of the children giggled.

Noah?

"Where's the flood, man?" the boy at the desk in front of me said.

"Mr. Epperson."

The boy looked back to see Mrs. Covey

n," he said. "So what?"
e do you get them?"
rother gives them to me. He steals
m my old man when he's drunk."
d was winning all the way around.
lo you keep blinking like that?" he

Tourette's syndrome."
ou catch that?"

" he said, looking more relaxed.
a Zippo lighter from his pocket,
pen its lid, and lit it.
everyone here so mean?" I asked.
lo you mean 'here'?" he asked.
h. They weren't mean in Califor-

e cigarette, then took a small puff.
e I know is mean," he said. He
ain, then coughed. "You sure you
t one?"
n't you get in trouble if they see

big deal. They'll just take my
I can get more. What's your

It doesn't stand for anything."
ng. I stood but B.J. just sat there.
ou going to class?" I asked.

glaring at him, her arms crossed at her chest.

"Do you have something to say to all of us?"

"No, ma'am."

She glanced at me once more, then breathed out heavily. "Back to work."

No one talked to me. An hour later I followed the kids to the cafeteria. My mother had forgotten to give me one of the lunch tickets she'd just purchased, so I just sat alone at the end of a table watching the other kids eat. Then, as the lunchroom cleared out, I wandered out to the playground. As I climbed up on the monkey bars, three boys walked up to me. I recognized one of them from my class.

"Hey, Noah. Where's the flood?"

I climbed down from the bars. The boys stood around me. One was almost a head taller than me. The middle boy was a redheaded kid who was the same height as me but huskier. The smallest of the three was shorter than me. He had small eyes and looked like a pig.

"Why does everyone keep asking me that?"

"He's such a dork he doesn't even know he's one," the redhead said.

"You can't swing on these," the biggest kid said.

"Why not?"

"Because I said so."

"Because he said so," Pig-face echoed. He took a step toward me. "You ever been in a fight before, dork?"

"No."

"You want to start something?"

"No."

"Why are you blinking like that?" the tall kid asked.

"I have tics," I said. "I can't help it."

"He's got bugs," the pig-faced kid said.

"Beat his bug face," the redhead said.

"Come on," Pig-face said. "Let's fight."

"I don't want to fight."

"What a chicken. I'm going to count to three. If you're still here, I'm going to break your nose."

I looked at the boys. They were enjoying this.

"I'll leave."

"Chicken," Pig-face said. He started clucking as I walked away.

I felt humiliated and angry. Most of all I hated my mother for leaving me here. This was the happy Utah my mother had gushed about.

I walked across the playground to the side of the school where I couldn't be seen. I sat down on the ground. I wanted to walk

home. My mother wo
I did, but the school
send the truancy offic
Just then a thin, ra
around the corner. H
me. He looked at m
sat down on the gras
ing floods?"
Everyone here wa
flood thing.
"What are floods?"
"It's what your pa
high. Look at 'em.
kles."
I still didn't un
"So?"
"It makes you loo
"Why do they cal
"Because they're
doesn't reach then
that I didn't kno
come from?"
"California."
He took a cigar
looked up at me.
"No."
"This is where
"You smoke cig
"Yeah."
"But you're, lik

"I'm t
"Wher
"My b
them fro
This ki
"Why
asked.
"I have
"Can y
"No."
"Good,
He took
flipped o
"Why is
"What
"In Uta
nia."
He lit th
"Everyone
inhaled ag
don't wan
"No. Wo
you?"
"It's no
cigarette.
name?"
"Rick."
"I'm B.J.
The bell ra
"Aren't y

"No."

I wished I could be that brave. "Okay."

"See you later," he said.

I walked back to class, falling in with the mass of children headed that way.

I learned three things that afternoon, none of them having anything to do with education. First, I wasn't safe. Two of the three boys who bullied me were in my class. Second, the big one was named Evan. And third, Mrs. Covey didn't like either her job or kids, and most likely neither. She treated our questions as annoyances and frequently rolled her eyes like we were all just stupid.

By the end of the day, I was pretty sure that I *was* stupid. And my mother was. She sent me to school without any school supplies. Shortly after we had returned from lunch, Mrs. Covey handed out some math worksheets, then walked around the class to watch us work. When she got to my desk she said, "Why aren't you writing anything down?"

"I don't have a pencil."

"You came to school without a pencil?" she said loud enough for the whole class to hear.

I could feel my face turning hot. "Yes, ma'am."

"They don't use pencils where you came

from, Mr. Evans?"

I wasn't sure if she meant it as a question.

"We used pencils," I said.

"Then you didn't think that we did?"

A few children giggled.

"No, ma'am. I mean, yes, ma'am." I wasn't sure how to answer that.

She breathed out heavily. "There are pencil machines in the front office," she said. "They're a nickel. Do you have a nickel?"

"No, ma'am. Not with me."

I had clearly pushed her to the limit of her patience. "Does anyone have a pencil they can loan Mr. Evans?"

The girl at the desk to the left of mine raised her hand. "I have an extra pencil."

"All right, Nancy. You may loan Mr. Evans a pencil."

The girl looked at me sympathetically as she handed me the pencil. It was pink and baby blue with a pink eraser and a cartoon of a unicorn on it.

"Thank you," I said.

"You owe Nancy a pencil," Mrs. Covey said. "Don't forget it."

After everyone had gone back to work, Mrs. Covey brought a stack of books over to my desk. "That's your math book, your history book, and your English book. Write your name in the front of each of them and don't lose them. If you lose them you have to pay for them."

There was a big round clock at the front of the room above Mrs. Covey's desk. If you looked closely you could see the minute hand slowly move. At a quarter after three the bell rang. Freedom.

"Don't forget your homework," Mrs. Covey said.

I stowed the textbooks in my desk, then escaped the room with the rest of the kids. I walked down the hallway ignoring still more comments about my floods and was relieved to get out of the place. On the way home I found two bottles, so I stopped at the Milk Depot for a peanut butter cup.

"You're dressed up," Cliff said.

"I had to go to school."

"So they finally got you, huh? What did you learn?"

"That it stinks."

He grinned. "Yeah, I never much liked it neither."

It took me about fifteen minutes to walk from school to home. My mother must have stopped at the store for school supplies because there were a notebook with lined paper, a half dozen pencils, and a large Pink Pearl eraser on the kitchen table. There was also a rucksack to carry my things in.

I didn't go to my mother's room. I was still mad at her. Instead, I got a bottle of peaches from the pantry and a fork, then walked out into the backyard to see my only friend. "Hey, Beau!" I shouted.

I could hear him barking as I neared the fence. To my dismay, my neighbor had already patched up the hole I'd made in it. I knelt down and put my hand under the fence. Beau licked my fingers.

"Do you know what a troll is?" I said. "Because I have one for a schoolteacher."

Beau just kept licking me.

Chapter 12

I stayed with Beau until it started to get dark. I could see that the light in the kitchen was on, which meant my mother was up. She smiled at me as I walked in. I was still angry at her betrayal.

"Dinner's on the table," she said. She had made a chicken broccoli casserole. She put a large scoop of it on my plate, then we sat down at the table.

"How was school?" she asked.

"I hate it."

She didn't look me in the eyes. "Sometimes we have to do things we don't like to do."

I didn't say anything. I still remembered her slap. After a few bites I said, "I don't think the people here are the same ones who lived here when you did. These people are mean. Especially Mrs. Covey. She's a troll."

"That's not a nice thing to say."

"*She's* the one that's not nice. She got

mad at me three times. That's all she does is get mad at kids."

"Maybe she was having a bad day."

"Maybe she's having a bad life."

My mother softly sighed. "Well, tomorrow's a new day."

I'm not sure what part of that was supposed to make me feel good. Maybe it wasn't.

"I have to get new pants for school," I said.

"What's wrong with the ones you have?"

"They're not long enough. Everyone made fun of me all day."

"Everyone?" She looked at me like I was exaggerating. I wasn't.

"Like a hundred times. They said, 'Where's the flood?' "

"What does that mean?"

"It means I look like a dork," I said.

She breathed out slowly. "I guess that won't do. We'll go this weekend."

Which meant I would spend the next three days fielding questions about my floods.

"When is Dad coming back?"

"I don't know," she said. "He . . ." She stopped and never finished. I wondered what she was going to say.

I ate about four bites of the casserole, then went to bed.

Chapter 13

While I was struggling with all the changes in my life, my mother just kept adding more. I think being back in her old home made her think she was supposed to live the way she did when she lived here. That included food.

The next morning for breakfast my mother made a bowl of something she called "gruel." It looked like a watered-down version of the paste we used (and secretly tasted) at school.

I took a bite. I wasn't sure what was worse, the texture or the taste.

"You can put bread in it," my mother said. "That's what I did when I was little."

I didn't. I had one more bite, then decided to skip breakfast.

"I need my lunch tickets," I said. "You never gave me any."

"What did you have for lunch yesterday?"

"I didn't eat."

She shook her head. "I'm so sorry. I forgot."

I didn't say anything.

Almost overnight I went from not knowing what day of the week it was to obsessing over it. The weekend was like a prison furlough. Saturday morning I got up early and watched TV. Nineteen sixty-seven was the golden age of Saturday morning cartoons: *Space Ghost, Casper the Friendly Ghost, Frankenstein Jr. and The Impossibles, The Fantastic Four,* and *The Herculoids,* with a triceratops that shot missiles from his horns. There was also *Shazzan* — a cartoon about two kids and a genie. It was presented by Mattel. (You can tell they're Mattel, because they're swell.)

It was a different culture back then, reflected in its cartoons. The villains had German or Russian accents and the superheroes, who were almost all white men, were either fighting futuristic space aliens or prehistoric dinosaurs, sometimes both in the same episode.

After making myself a breakfast of cinnamon toast, I watched cartoons for most of the morning, then, when the cartoons ended, I went out to the garage to work on my robot. I fantasized about making him strong enough to beat up Evan and his cronies. At least it could shock them.

Later that afternoon it began to snow for the first time. I had never seen an actual snowfall or witnessed the landscape change before me. I stood in the front yard watching it for nearly a half hour. It was magical. When I went inside, my mother made us hot chocolate. It was a rare, pleasant moment.

The next morning the snow in our yard was nearly two feet high. For a boy raised in California it was like being on a different planet. I had plans. First I'd check on Beau, then I'd make a snowman. The idea of rolling a ball of snow around the yard was very appealing.

As I was getting ready to go out, my mother called for me. "Ricky." (She was the only one who still called me that.)

I walked to her room. "Yes?"

"It snowed last night."

"I know," I said. "It snowed a *lot.*"

"I need you to shovel the driveway so I can get the car out. There's a snow shovel in the garage."

When had she been in the garage? I thought.

"Do you think you could do that?"

I had never shoveled snow before — I didn't even know that it was a thing — but it sounded grown-up. "Yes."

"Be sure to dress warmly."

I didn't really have any warm clothes, just a Levi's jacket. I put it on with my sneakers and some knit gloves my mother had. They were pink and baby blue, like an Easter dress, and I didn't really want to wear them, but my mother insisted with the puzzling warning, "You could get frostbite without them."

Snow bit? This place got stranger all the time.

"We'll get you some gloves and a winter coat today," she said. "But first we need to get out of the driveway."

The snow was almost up to my knees as I walked out to the garage. The snow shovel was near the door. It looked simple enough: a long wooden pole connected to a curved metal blade. *Like raking leaves,* I thought. *How hard could this be?*

I immediately discovered how much heavier snow was than leaves, and shoveling it wasn't nearly as much fun as I thought it would be.

As I was shoveling, I heard Beau's bark and I looked over at my neighbor's house. The old man had come out on his porch. He looked at the snow for a minute, pushed his cane into it to measure it, then glanced over at me. I quickly turned away, pretending not to see him. The two of them went back inside.

When I was mostly done, my mother came out in a long wool coat and boots. She was carrying a broom.

"We really got a lot of snow," she said. "I'm sorry there's not two shovels. I'll finish up here."

She looked too weak to me. "That's okay," I said. "I'll do it."

She smiled. "Thank you."

It took me another twenty minutes to finish. I wondered if my father had to shovel snow where he was.

CHAPTER 14

After I had cleared the snow from the driveway, we got into the station wagon and drove to JCPenney for school clothes. My mother bought me a sweatshirt with Snoopy on it and two long pairs of jeans. Also, some snow boots and gloves.

My mother looked especially concerned as she looked over the coats. I showed her the one I liked, but she glanced at the price tag and, without saying anything, hung it back up. We ended up with a coat that was "big enough for me to grow into," which meant it didn't fit me now, the sleeves falling two inches past my knuckles.

After that my mother let me go into the mall's pet shop to look at the animals, which, to me, was like a miniature version of the zoo. When we got back home it had finally stopped snowing.

"Poor Mr. Foster is snowed in," my mother said. "I hope he doesn't have to go anywhere."

I walked into the house thinking about our neighbor's plight, then put on my new coat and gloves and dragged the shovel over to his house. It took me nearly an hour to shovel his walk. I was exhausted. He never came out. I hoped he might forgive me for cutting the hole in his fence.

Chapter 15

Monday, October 23

It was a little over a week before Halloween and Mrs. Covey gave us some Halloween-themed art projects that lessened the existential pain of being in her class. It was also time for our show-and-tell. I thought of bringing my robot, but part of me didn't want to share it. It wasn't ready yet, and I didn't want to subject it to possible ridicule. I thought of bringing the telephone magneto and shocking everyone, but then feared that someone might steal it, leaving my robot defenseless. What I really wanted to bring was Beau, but I knew that wasn't going to happen. With the snow, he didn't play out in the yard as much, and I missed him. I ended up bringing a seashell I'd found on Long Beach a few years earlier.

A girl named Corinne brought a robin's nest her father had taken down from a tree in their yard. It had a tiny blue egg inside.

There was a handwritten sign next to it that said DON'T TOUCH, which to a fourth grader was tantamount to a command. I did what any normal kid would do — I pressed my finger to it. To my horror, the egg broke. Blood rushed to my face. I looked around. Fortunately, no one saw me do it, so I skulked back to my seat, certain I'd be executed if I were caught.

I watched, out of the corner of my eye, as my crime was discovered. Corinne was very upset. She told Mrs. Covey, who stood before the class.

"Someone broke Corinne's egg. Who touched her egg?"

I was burning with guilt. I wanted to confess, but Mrs. Covey was so angry, only a fool would throw themselves in front of that train.

Later that afternoon, in English, Mrs. Covey taught us about idioms. An idiom is a phrase or expression that usually represents a nonliteral meaning. Like *bite the bullet* or *hit the sack,* two idioms my father used to say a lot.

Our assignment was to make a list of ten idioms. I wrote down these ten.

That's the last straw.
You're pulling my leg.

You missed the boat.
Back to the drawing board.
Get your act together.
Piece of cake.
Break the ice.
Hang in there.
Cutting corners.
Don't rain on my parade.

English had always been my favorite subject, and assignments like this were a piece of cake. (See what I did there?) I finished my paper by writing my name at the top of the page.

Rick Evans

I don't know what possessed me at that moment, but in a sudden and impetuous act of pretension, I added something to my name.

Rick Evans *the great*

I don't know why I wrote it. The truth was, I felt anything but great. But for a few seconds, it felt good — like maybe I was worth more than I thought I was. I left the paper on Mrs. Covey's desk and happily walked home for the day.

Chapter 16

Tuesday, October 24

The following afternoon we got our papers back. Mrs. Covey had given me a D on the assignment, the lowest grade I had ever received on any of my work. I couldn't understand why she had given me such a bad grade. Then I realized it had nothing to do with the assignment. It was the addition I had made to my name.

Mrs. Covey had erased the two extraneous words and replaced them with three of her own.

Shame on you

After the papers had all been handed out, Mrs. Covey stood before the class. She looked angry, which she usually did, but today she looked particularly cross.

"Yesterday I gave you an assignment to write down ten idioms. I'd like to share with you a few idioms that came to mind as I graded one of your papers. How about *too big for his britches, full of himself, stuck up,* or *has a swelled head.*

"One of you turned a paper in yesterday. Apparently, this classmate of yours had such a high opinion of himself, that he wrote next to his name . . ."

She turned back to the chalkboard and said, as she wrote it, "The Great."

I felt my face flush with embarrassment. My cheek began twitching.

"Are there any great men or women in the room? If so, please raise your hand."

No one raised their hand.

"Oh? But one of you wrote this. Have you changed your mind?" She looked at me. I was paralyzed with shame.

"So, as I looked at this paper, I asked myself, why would someone go to the trouble to write this about himself. What is it to be great?" She paused for emphasis. "I would define a great person as one who has made a significant contribution to solving the world's problems. Would that describe any of you? Did any of you solve world hunger today? Stop a war?" Her gaze again ended on me. "I didn't think so."

"If that's the case, then I can only think of one reason someone would write that next to his name." She turned back to the chalk-board and wrote, in twelve-inch letters:

HUBRIS

"H-U-B-R-I-S," she said, enunciating each letter. "Hubris. Does anyone know what that means?"

Crickets.

"It's an ugly word with many synonyms. Conceit. Arrogance. Insolence. High-mindedness. Haughtiness. Shall I go on?"

Still no one answered.

"*Hubris* is another word for pride. What does pride mean? Anyone?"

Nancy raised her hand.

"Yes, Nancy."

"It means to be proud."

"Thank you, Nancy, for providing us with an answer that explains absolutely nothing. Class, what does it mean to be proud?"

Nothing. I felt bad for Nancy. She didn't need Mrs. Covey to feel bad about herself. The kids made fun of her because someone said that she came over for a sleepover and wet the bed.

"Here's another definition," the crone said. "To be proud means to hold a high opinion of oneself or one's importance." She looked around the room. "Do we have any *important* people in this room?"

Again, nothing.

"Really? No Nobel Prize winners in the room? No millionaires? No great scientists? No great explorers? I'll even take a rock-and-roll musician." She again looked around the room. "Hmm. It's a shame. I was rather excited to meet this important young man."

How long is this going to go on? I wondered. I wanted to bolt.

"Pride tops the list of the most sinful of the deadly sins. Pride goes before destruction, a haughty spirit before a fall. So, to you who thought to call himself great, I warn you, it is a very dangerous path you tread. One that the very devil himself followed to become the devil."

I shouldn't have been surprised at how well she knew the devil and his history. I could see the two of them sitting around drinking coffee together, bragging about who brought about the most misery.

Mrs. Covey finally let out a long sigh of disgust.

"All right, Mr. Great, you've wasted enough of your classmates' time. Everyone take out your math assignment."

With all that was going wrong in my life, I had suspected that God hated me, but Mrs. Covey had confirmed it. I was on par with the devil himself.

After her lengthy diatribe, every minute of class felt like an hour. I just wanted to go home and never come back.

As I was walking out of school someone shouted, "Hey, Ricky, you think you're great, huh?"

I looked back. It was Evan and his demonic duo.

"No."

"You think you're better than us? Don't you?"

"No."

"Then why'd you write it?"

I didn't answer.

"I asked you a question, dork."

"Who said I wrote it?"

"Everyone knows you wrote it, moron. Covey was talking to you the whole time."

It *was* pretty obvious that she was. Even Evan and his band of miscreants could figure it out.

"Because I wanted to," I said.

"Covey says you're the devil," Evan said.

"She said I was on the same path as the devil. And you're following me, so what does that make you?"

Flustered, Evan shouted, "Get him!"

I took off running. Fearing for my life, I did probably the most foolish and dangerous thing I could have done: I darted across Thirty-Third south, a busy four-lane road. A car slid sideways to miss me. The driver laid on his horn. "You idiot kid!" he shouted, shaking his fist.

I wasn't an especially fast runner, but I was pretty scared, which is how I had almost made it home when Evan tackled me in Mr. Foster's front yard, my face plowing through the deep snow. My rucksack flew off my shoulder. All three of them jumped on me, shoving snow in my face and down my coat and pants.

"We're going to beat the devil out of you," Evan said. "Ricky the Great." He shoved snow up my nose. I couldn't shout. I couldn't even breathe. I thought I might pass out.

Suddenly Evan cried out in pain. I heard a gruff voice say, "Get off."

Pig-face shouted, "It's the old Negro!"

Evan groaned again, then shouted, "I'm getting off. I'm getting off."

He rolled off me onto his back, his hands crossed at his face. "Don't hit me."

I turned around to see my neighbor standing above both of us, holding a wooden cane above him like a Louisville Slugger. Evan's two friends had already taken off running.

I looked back and forth between Evan and

Mr. Foster.

"Do I need to crack open your skull, boy, and fill it with brains?" he said to Evan.

"No, sir."

He lowered the cane to point it at him. "Now you listen to me," the man said in a low voice. "And you listen well. I know where you live, Evan. If I hear you're bullying my friend again, I'll come to your house in the middle of the night, and no one will ever hear or see you again. Do you understand?"

Evan's eyes were as wide as silver dollars. "Yes, sir."

"Don't you forget that. Because if I have to come for you, I won't have time to hear you begging for mercy. This is your mercy right now. Next time will be too late." He lifted the cane again. "Are you sure you understand?"

Evan was shaking. "Yes, sir."

"Then get off my property."

Evan got up and ran off as fast as he could.

Mr. Foster watched him go, then looked back down at me. "Are you okay?"

I wiped my face with the sleeve of my coat. It was red with blood and snot. I lifted myself up on my elbows. "Yes," I said, even though I wasn't.

He lifted my rucksack from the snow.

"That snow is going to ruin your books. What's wrong with those boys?" He looked me over, then said, "You must be cold. Come inside and get warm."

The cold was almost imperceptible with all the other pain I felt. My nose was still bleeding, and my eye felt like it was swelling up. But that was nothing compared to the humiliation and fear I felt. Truth be told, I was just as afraid of this old Black man as I was of Evan and his demonic friends. Luckily for me, I was too afraid to run.

CHAPTER 17

Mr. Foster grabbed the sleeve of my coat and lifted me up.

"Your name is Richard," he said. I didn't know how he knew that.

"My mom calls me Rick."

"I like Richard. It's the name of nobility. Come on in."

I followed him up the walk to his house, stomping the snow from my feet as he opened the door.

"Don't worry about my dog," he said. "He doesn't bite. He's just friendly." He looked at me. "You already know that, don't you."

"Yes, sir."

As I stepped inside Beau jumped up on me, his tail wagging frantically.

"Get off him, Gollum," Mr. Foster said, shutting the door behind us.

"He's okay," I said, crouching down to pet him. Beau started licking my hand.

The front of his home was open, with the

front room and dining room connected and the kitchen separated only by a bar. It had a pleasant and rich ambience. There was Christmas music playing, like the backdrop of a holiday movie. I thought this was a little peculiar since it wasn't even November yet. My parents wouldn't bring out the Christmas albums until Thanksgiving.

Not that I was complaining. I liked it. The house smelled like baking cookies.

"I've seen you back there with Gollum."

"I didn't know your dog's name," I said. "I've been calling him Beau."

"Beau is a better name. It means handsome in French."

"What's a Gollum?"

His brow furrowed. "Haven't you read *The Hobbit* by Mr. J. R. R. Tolkien?"

"No, sir."

"You're fortunate you have that to look forward to. Gollum's a creature, of sorts. But it wouldn't do justice for me to explain him. The truth is, it doesn't matter much what you call him. He'll answer to just about anything. You can call him Beau."

"He sticks his nose under the fence to lick my hand."

"He's always looking for a new friend. Squirrels, cats, anything that moves. He's always trying to get out to play. That's why

I'm always fixing that fence." He looked at me. "Was that you who cut a hole in my fence?"

I knew that he knew it was me. I started twitching. "I'm sorry. I just wanted to pet Beau."

He looked at me for a moment, then said, "I'm not angry. I was just afraid he would get out. He's a wanderer. I should have named him Marco Polo. He got out once and I found him in the middle of Thirty-Third."

He took off his coat and hung it on a coatrack. Then he walked over to the kitchen, got a dishrag and ran water over it, then brought it back to me. "You can wipe your face with this," he said. "You've still got some blood on it."

"Thank you." I held the cloth to my face. "What kind of dog is Beau?"

"The troublesome kind." He looked at me. "You want to know what breed he is."

"Yes, sir."

"He's half King Charles Cavalier spaniel, half something fuzzy." He pointed to a big chair with an ottoman. "Have a seat in my chair."

"Okay." I set the bloodstained cloth on the table, then sat down. Beau jumped up in my lap.

"Before that pack of boys brought you down, I put a tray of cookies in the oven. Would you like a hot cookie?"

"Yes, sir."

"They're still baking. I'll make you some hot cocoa to warm your bones."

He took the teakettle over to the sink and filled it with water, set it on the stove, then began tidying up his kitchen.

I petted Beau while I looked around the room. The house might have been built around the same time as my grandmother's, but it was in a lot better condition. It had an eclectic but deliberate design. The room's floor was carpeted in a bright red shag and the walls were covered with pale blue wallpaper with slightly darker blue floral patterns running down in vertical lines. There were long, navy blue floor-to-ceiling curtains.

On one wall there was a collection of photographs in elaborate gold frames with black-and-white photographs inside them. Mr. Foster was much younger and thinner in all the photographs. There was one of him in a sailor's uniform standing on the deck of a ship. In another he was standing next to a woman and a small boy in front of an old Plymouth automobile.

"Is that your family?"

"That's my wife, Margaret, and my son."

"How old is your son?"

"In that picture, he's just a little younger than you. He was six. But that was a long time ago."

"I just turned nine two weeks ago," I said.

"Happy birthday."

I looked back at the picture. The boy was standing between his parents and had a big smile. "What's his name?"

"Isaiah. Like the prophet."

"Where does he live?"

"He's with his mother."

"How come they're not with you?"

"We're separated."

"Oh," I said softly. "My parents are separated."

"I'm sorry to hear that." He looked genuinely sad. "It's hard being apart. But I'm going to see my family this Christmas. I am very much looking forward to that."

Next to the armchair there was a tall wooden bookshelf filled with books. To the side of it was a Magnavox television and record player console. It was playing Nat King Cole's "The Christmas Song." I could see the colorful album sleeve on the floor leaning up against one of the console's legs.

In the corner of the room was a small bluish-green spruce Christmas tree. It was sparse of limb, with gaping spaces between each layer of boughs. A long red tinsel garland wrapped around the tree and the boughs had been generously draped with silver tinsel along with bright red and green baubles. I wondered where he'd gotten a Christmas tree so early.

"You already have a Christmas tree."

"Yes. I always put it up early. I love Christmas. It's my favorite time of the year."

"Mine too," I said.

The teakettle began to whistle. Mr. Foster took it from the stove and set it on a cold burner as its scream faded. "Come sit at the table."

I set Beau on the floor, then walked to the table. Beau followed me over. Mr. Foster brought me a porcelain coffee cup and filled it with steaming water.

"My mother makes cocoa with milk," I said.

"This is a different kind of cocoa. You'll like it." He took an envelope out of a blue box, tore open the envelope, and poured the cocoa powder into the cup. "The milk is already in it, so you just add water." He pushed the cup across the table to me, then handed me a spoon. "You have to stir the powder in until it all dissolves. Be careful, it's hot."

I stirred the cocoa for nearly a minute, then took a sip. It tasted surprisingly creamy. A tinny bell on the oven began ringing.

"That's our cookies," he said. He walked over to the oven and opened the door. "Yes, just right." He put on an oven mitt and pulled out the cookie sheet. The smell of the cookies filled the room. The cookies were in the shape of Christmas trees and had been sprinkled with green sugar.

"There is nothing more delicious than a classic sugar cookie. Just eggs, flour, vanilla, butter, and sugar."

"They smell good," I said.

"You haven't tasted them yet." He lifted the cookies with a spatula and put them on waxed paper. "Is your mama going to be happy with all this sugar I'm feeding you?" he asked.

"We don't have a lot of sweets at home."

"Then we'll just keep it a secret," he said. He put several cookies on a plate and brought them over to the table. "Careful with that, they're still hot."

I picked up a cookie, blew on it, then took a bite. It tasted even better than it smelled. After I had eaten a whole cookie, I looked up at him. "You said you would go to Evan's house at night. Would you really do that?"

"No. I don't know where that boy lives. I

didn't even know his name until I heard his friends shout it. But he doesn't know that. That's all that matters. I didn't want them coming back at you when I wasn't around."

"I don't know why they hate me."

"They don't hate you. Bullying people makes them feel strong. And that feels special. Everyone wants to feel special. Even you."

"That's a stupid way to feel special."

"I don't disagree. There are two ways of being strong: one is pushing people down, the other is pulling people up."

"You pulled me up."

"So I did."

"What's your name?" I asked.

"Booker. You can call me that if your parents let you call adults by their first name. If not, you can call me Mr. Foster."

"They don't like me to call adults by their first names."

He nodded. "I noticed you say 'Yes, sir' and 'No, sir.' Your parents have raised you to be respectful," he said. "That's a good thing — a rare thing these days."

"Did your parents call you Booker because you like books?"

"I don't think I liked books before I was born, which is when my name was chosen. But maybe my mama had a premonition.

You're not wrong about me liking books. I'm what they call a bibliophile. Books are an important part of my life."

The way he was talking reminded me of my brother. "My brother was always trying to get me to read."

"Your brother is smart. Books are powerful things. They give you knowledge, and knowledge gives you power. But that's not why my mama gave me that name. She named me after a man she admired named Mr. Booker T. Washington. Do you know who that is?"

I shook my head.

"Mr. Washington was a very smart and very wise man. Mind you, those are not the same thing. The world is full of educated people who aren't wise. They might mean well, but they get us in a lot of trouble.

"Mr. Washington liked books, too. He once said, 'If you can't read, it's going to be hard to realize your dreams.' "

"I don't like to read," I said.

"You probably just haven't found the right books to read. The ones that speak to you."

"I've never heard a book speak," I said.

"You've never read a book that made you want to be different?"

"There's a book about robots I liked. My teacher read it to us."

"I thought so." He walked across the room to his bookshelf. He took out a book and brought it back to me. "This is the book Mr. Washington wrote about himself."

The book was titled *Up from Slavery.* I looked it over, then gave it back to him. He set it on the table.

"Where did you come here from?" he asked.

"California."

"Whereabout in California?"

"Pasadena."

"Pasadena," he echoed. "Such nice weather there. I especially like those palm trees. You said you have a brother?"

"I had a brother."

"You *had* a brother?"

"Yes, sir. He was killed in Vietnam."

His expression fell. "I'm very sorry for your loss. Did that have something to do with you moving here?"

"I think so. My dad lost his job after my brother died, so we had to sell our house. There was no one in my grandma's house so they said we could live here."

"I knew your grandma," he said. "She was a good woman. For years we had a mutually beneficial arrangement. I'd grow the berries and bring them to her, and she'd make preserves out of them. I still have a whole cabinet full of them."

"We have a lot of jam at our house, too," I said.

"Good thing you told me. I was going to send some home with you."

I finished drinking my cocoa and started on another cookie.

"How is your eye feeling?"

"It hurts."

"I'm afraid you're going to get a shiner. If you hold some snow to your eye, it won't swell as much. You probably should get on home before your mama starts to worry."

"She doesn't worry," I said.

"Every mother worries. Especially when she sees that shiner on your face."

"She doesn't come out of her room at night."

His brow fell. "Is she a drinker?"

"No. She just gets a lot of headaches."

"Did she have them before your brother died?"

"No."

He nodded. "I understand." He lightly sighed. "Let me send some of these cookies home with you." He put most of the cookies into a paper sack, then grabbed a loaf of bread from the counter and gave them both to me. "I baked that bread this morning. It's sourdough from my own starter. Tell your mama it's a gift from Mr. Foster. If she likes it, I'll bake her more."

"Okay."

"Wait. One more thing. He walked to his bookshelf and brought down another book. "Here you go. *The Hobbit.*" He put the book in the rucksack along with my textbooks. "There, you're all loaded up now."

He lifted Beau, then opened the front door for me. "It was a pleasure meeting you, Mr. Richard."

"Me too," I said awkwardly. I stepped out onto the porch.

"Richard."

I turned back. "Yes?"

"Thank you for shoveling my driveway. That was very kind of you."

"You're welcome."

"If you like, you can stop by on the way home from school tomorrow. Beau and I are baking thumbprint cookies. You can help us bake them. I'll teach you how."

I had no idea what the thumbprint part of a cookie was, but he had me at "cookie." And learning how to bake was even better.

"Okay."

"Very well, then. We'll see you tomorrow."

It was already starting to get dark as I walked the short distance to my house, my arms full of the things Mr. Foster had sent me home with. Unlike Mr. Foster's home, our home was cold and silent.

"I'm home," I said as I walked in. There was no response. I set everything on the kitchen table, took off my coat, then walked to my mother's bedroom and opened her door. As usual the room was dark. My mother was lying in bed with a cold pack on her forehead. "Hi, honey," she said softly. "How was your day?"

Fortunately, she couldn't see my face.

"It was okay."

"What time is it?"

"I don't know. It's dark."

"Where have you been?"

"Exploring."

She didn't question this.

"Did Dad call today?"

"No. Do you have homework?"

"A little."

"Get it done before you watch television. There's some Bean with Bacon soup on the stove for dinner. You'll have to reheat it."

"Okay."

I walked back to the dining area. After all the cookies I'd eaten, I wasn't really hungry. I took the book Mr. Foster had given me out of the rucksack and opened it up.

In a hole in the ground there lived a hobbit. Not a nasty, dirty, wet hole, filled with the ends of worms and an oozy smell, nor yet a dry, bare, sandy hole with nothing in it to sit down on or to eat: it was a hobbit-hole, and that means comfort.

I read until I fell asleep with the book next to me.

Three things changed for me that night. For the first time I discovered the joy of reading. Evan and his cronies never bullied me again. And I never felt so alone again.

Chapter 18

The next morning, I was in the bathroom examining my black eye in the mirror when my mother called from the dining room. "Ricky, where did this food come from?"

I was hoping that she wouldn't get out of bed this morning. I knew she would respond angrily when she saw my black eye. I walked out to her. She didn't disappoint. She looked over my swollen eye, then asked, "What happened?"

"Some boys beat me up."

"What boys?"

"Some boys in my class."

Her face flushed with anger. "Okay, I'm driving you to school. I'm going to have a talk with your principal."

I didn't want to go through the embarrassment of that. Besides, I was more afraid of the principal than I was of Evan. I'd seen him bully students and teachers. He had a thing about kids not finishing their school lunches. Sometimes he'd come into the lunchroom and stand by the tray return to make sure the kids had eaten everything on their tray. Once, a boy didn't like some of the food, so he thought he could sneak it by the principal by stuffing it all together into his milk carton. The principal caught him. He made him dump it out and eat it.

"It won't help," I said. "At this school they give extra credit for bullying."

She wasn't amused. "That's not going to happen on my watch."

"They're not going to beat me up again."

"You don't know that."

"Mr. Foster told them if they ever bully me again, he would go after them. He told me to tell you we've got this covered."

She looked perplexed. "Mr. Foster next door?"

I nodded.

"Is that where all this food came from?"

"He gave it to us. He said the bread is a gift for you. If you like it, he'll bake us some more."

She still looked perplexed. "How did all this come about?"

"The boys were beating me up in Mr. Foster's front yard and he came out and stopped them."

She looked at me for a moment, then

sighed. "If that's what you w
we'll just see what happens."

"Can I have toast with jam for

"Of course." She took the loa
into the kitchen.

The kids at school all looked at m
was a freak with my black eye. All c
except Evan and his friends. They
look at me at all, which was fine by m

Even Mrs. Covey noticed. She was r
ing her rounds and stopped at my desk.
looked at me curiously, then just contin
without a word.

At lunchtime I sat behind the school wi
my book. As usual, B.J. showed up with a
pack of his father's cigarettes. Benson &
Hedges. He sat down on the grass next t
me and lit a cigarette.

"What happened to your eye?" he aske

"I got beat up."

"There's a lot of that here." He to
drag from his cigarette, then blew it
"Whatcha reading?"

I waved the smoke from my fac
book."

"What book?"

I held it up. *"The Hobbit."*

"Is it any good?"

"Yeah. Do you like to read?"

e took another drag, then said, "Yeah. I d all the time."

didn't expect that.

was unusually happy that day, for two asons. First, I wasn't afraid that I was go-g to be bullied, and second, I had some-ing to look forward to. Cookies and Beau.

s soon as the bell rang, I threw my ruck-ack over my shoulder and ran home. I walked up to Mr. Foster's house and rang the doorbell. Mr. Foster opened the door while Beau yapped at his feet.

"I came," I said.

"I can see that." He was staring at my black eye. "What a nice shiner that turned out to be."

"It's not nice," I said.

"No, it's not. Come in. Don't let Beau out."

I noticed that he called him Beau instead of Gollum. I walked inside slightly bent over, my hands on Beau to keep him from escaping. I shut the door behind me and ooked up. There were large cookie sheets n the table, next to a big bowl.

"Wash your hands." He smiled. "We don't ant Beau all over our cookies." He looked own at Beau. "No offense, dog."

went to the sink and washed my hands.

Let's get started. First thing, we grease

the pans. These cookies already have a lot of butter in them, so not too much."

He took a dishcloth and pressed it into a can of Crisco, then lightly rubbed it over the sheet.

"Next we roll the dough into balls." He reached into the bowl and brought out a small piece of dough. He rolled it in his hands until it was about the size of a golf ball.

"Just like that," he said. "You try it."

I took a piece of dough out of the bowl.

"A little more than that," he said.

I brought out a little more, then rolled it between my hands.

"Very nice," he said. "You've done this before."

"With Play-Doh," I said.

He nodded. "Dough is dough. At least until you eat it."

"Play-Doh isn't sweet," I said.

"Every kid has to try it," he said.

I rolled the entire bowl of dough into small balls, setting them on the counter in front of me.

"Before we put them on the cookie sheets, I like to roll the cookies in sugar. It gives them more crunch and a little glitter." He set a bowl filled with granulated sugar in front of me. I rolled each of the balls in the sugar, then he showed me how to distance them on the cookie sheet.

"Now we make the thumbprint. Give me your hand." I reached out my hand and he took my thumb and pressed it in the middle of one of the dough balls, like a policeman taking a fingerprint. "Just like that," he said. "It flattens the cookie and gives us a nice little reservoir to put our filling in. Just like gravy in mashed potatoes. Just don't push down too much."

I pushed my thumb into each of the balls until they were all flat.

"Very good. Now, we can bake them like this, or we can put the filling in first. I prefer to put the filling in before baking them." He had several bottles of fruit preserves on the counter. He took a teaspoon of apricot jam and spooned it onto the cookie. "These are your grandma's preserves," he said. "Do you want to try?"

"Yes."

He handed me the spoon. "You'll need a heaping spoonful."

I took out some jam and put it on a cookie. It was messy but he praised me anyway. "That's right. Just like that." As I was filling the rest of the cookies he said, "I have so many jars of your grandma's preserves that I usually use those. But you can

put other things in the cookie."
"Like what?"
"Like chocolate."
I looked up at him. "Can we try chocolate?"
"You like chocolate, do you?" He took a bag of Brach's chocolate stars down from a cabinet. "We'll use these. You can have some. Just don't let Beau have any. Chocolate's not good for dogs."
I took out a chocolate and popped it into my mouth.
"Good, huh?"
I nodded. He took several stars from the bag and put them in the cookies, then he slid one of the sheets into the oven.
"Now we bake."
I sat down at the table.
"How was school today?"
"It was fine."
"Did anyone notice your black eye?"
"Everyone noticed it."
"I'm not surprised. How about those boys? Any trouble with them?"
"They stayed away from me."
"Good." He smiled. "I'd hate to have to pay them a visit."
It was about fifteen minutes more before the oven timer rang. "Let's check on those," he said. With some difficulty, he pushed

himself up from the table. He opened the oven.

"Just right. You don't want them to brown on top." He grabbed an oven mitt and took out the sheet, setting it on an oven pad on the counter. "Don't those look delicious. Look how the sugar glistens."

They did look good. The chocolate stars had melted perfectly into my thumb's imprint.

"Now we let them sit a moment." He put in the second cookie sheet and sat back down. "Did you open that book I sent you home with?"

I nodded. "Yes."

"And?"

"I'm at the part where the company gets lost in the forest. It's scary."

He chuckled with delight. "Lost in Mirkwood forest. I told you, you've just been reading the wrong books. So you've met Gollum."

"He's creepy."

"He is creepy. Mr. Tolkien writes a lot more about him in his later books."

"Why did you call Beau Gollum?"

Mr. Foster grinned. "I was just amusing myself." He looked down at Beau. "He's my *precious.*"

The bell on the oven rang and Mr. Foster

took out the second batch of cookies. He set them on the counter next to the other sheet.

"Where is your father these days?"

"He lives with a friend."

"Do you see much of him?"

"No. My mom says he's busy with his new job."

"I'm sure your mama's right."

After I had eaten a dozen of the small cookies, Mr. Foster said, "That's enough for now. You should get on home to your mama."

I got up from the table. "See you, Beau."

"I'll send some cookies home with you." He winked. "For your mama."

"Thanks. My mom says thank you for the bread. She really liked it."

"Tell her that the next time I bake I'll make a few extra loaves." He looked at me. "Speaking of baking, if you like, you can come by on Saturday. Beau and I will be baking again."

"What time?" I asked.

"Around noon."

"Okay."

I walked home with a Tupperware full of cookies, a full stomach, and a growing friendship.

Chapter 19

Saturday, October 28

Saturday morning I didn't even finish watching my usual lineup of cartoons before I walked over to Mr. Foster's house.

"King Richard," Mr. Foster said, smiling, as he opened the door. Beau was in his arms, barking excitedly. "Beau's happy to see you. Come on in."

I stepped inside. As usual, I could smell something baking.

"We're baking croissants."

"What's that?"

"These right here." On the kitchen table there were trays of dough twisted into crescents. Some of them were already baked. They were golden-brown, glossy on top.

"They're French rolls in the shape of a crescent. They were originally Austrian, but the French stole the recipe and made it their own. There are few things in this world as tasty as a hot butter-puff croissant."

"Why are they shiny like that?"

"That's an old baker's trick my mama taught me," he said. "I whisk up an egg with a little cream and brush it on before I bake it. It's called an egg wash. It makes it more fancy-looking."

"Why are you making so many?"

"Every Saturday I bake something up for the homeless shelter downtown. They send someone over to pick it up.

"Since your mama liked my bread, I baked a few extra croissants for you to take home. There's a basket in that closet you can put them in. It's on the shelf to the left."

I opened the closet door. The narrow space was crowded with stacked wooden Coca-Cola crates filled with empty bottles. Several of the stacks were taller than me. It looked like a gold mine. The mother lode. Sometimes it took me twenty minutes to find a single empty bottle.

"You've got a lot of empty bottles in here."

"I know. They've gotten a little out of hand."

"If you take them to the Milk Depot, they'll give you money for them," I said. "A nickel apiece."

"I know. But it's too much work for me to take them down these days, so I've just let them stack up the last few years."

I brought the breadbasket out of the closet and took it over to the table.

"Tell you what," he said, as he filled the basket with rolls. "I'll make you a business arrangement. If you take those bottles in, I'll split the deposit money with you. Does that sound fair?"

It sounded a lot more than fair. "Yes."

"All right, then. It's a deal. Let's get them moving."

"Right now?"

"There's never a time like the present."

"I need to go home and get a bag to carry them."

"You'll need more than a bag. I have a wagon around back you can use. Just pull it up to the back door."

I walked out the back door. The wagon was what he used for his garden. It was green with wood-slat sides and had a bent black metal handle. It was filled with a bag of fertilizer, work gloves, and all sorts of garden implements.

"Just empty everything out there on the ground," Mr. Foster said from the doorway.

I took everything out of the wagon, then pulled it up to the back door. Mr. Foster propped the door open while I started carrying out all the soda and milk bottles.

me a favor? Beau's not been out today. Could you take him with you?"

"Sure," I said. I was thrilled with the idea. I think Mr. Foster knew I would be, since he had already put a leash on him.

"C'mon, Beau," I said. I threaded my wrist through the loop on the leash, then headed off. It wasn't as easy as I expected, since Beau had to inspect every stick he passed, and he stopped twice to pee, but I was glad for his company. He made me laugh.

Cliff asked, "Who's your friend, there?"

"That's Beau," I said. "He's Mr. Foster's dog."

"Looks like he's your dog."

"I wish he was my dog."

He cashed out the last of my bottles, then handed me a package of Reese's Peanut Butter Cups. "Here's a little something on the house. It's a pleasure doing business with you."

Beau and I walked back to the house with the rest of the money. I set the last payment on the table along with the peanut butter cups.

"What's this?" Mr. Foster asked, lifting the candy.

"Cliff gave it to us for all the bottles we took him."

He set the package in front of me. "That's all yours. He gave it to you as a tip for all your hard work." He settled back in his chair. "So, partner, let's see what we've got here." He picked up the money and shuffled through it. "There's twenty-seven dollars here; divided fifty-fifty, that comes to thirteen dollars and fifty cents for each of us."

I couldn't believe my good fortune. He handed me two fives, three ones, and five dimes. "And," he said, lifting a dollar from his stack, "here's a dollar for taking Beau on a walk."

"You don't have to pay me to walk Beau."

"I know," he said. "You're very kind that way. But I was hoping that maybe we could make another arrangement and I could pay you one dollar to walk him every day. Except Sunday, of course. Beau needs a day of rest, too. Would that arrangement be satisfactory to you?"

"Yes, sir."

"And, if I might push my luck, I'm too old to push that snow shovel anymore. I'm afraid I'm going to get buried in here someday. So, if it's okay by you, I'll pay you three dollars to shovel my driveway and walkway every time it snows. Does that sound fair?"

"Yes, sir."

"Wonderful. This is a most pleasing arrangement. Let's celebrate our arrangement with some hot croissants."

I ate five of the rolls. They were hot and chewy and flaky, basically the most delicious bread-things I had ever had. I ate three of them with strawberry preserves.

I stayed at Mr. Foster's home all afternoon. I opened the door when the people from the homeless shelter came and got the rolls. As it started to get dark, Mr. Foster said, "You better get on home. Your mama's going to be worried."

"Okay." I crouched down to the floor. "Bye, Beau. I'll see you tomorrow."

I walked home with fourteen dollars and fifty cents in my pocket. I had never been so rich in my life. And, with our new arrangement, I would be stinking rich by Christmas. I remember thinking it was a good thing my parents had given me that safe for my birthday.

Chapter 20

Monday, October 30

At school I was starting to be friends with one of my classmates, a redheaded boy named Jed. He was quiet like me, though he always seemed a little sad. I found out later that his father had died over the summer. We would sit together at lunch, then go out and play marbles. That was the big thing at this school. Kids would pick games with each other, the winner confiscating the loser's marble. Jed and I just played for fun. We never took each other's marbles.

We had played for a while when Jed said, "Evan doesn't bully you anymore."

"I know."

"He doesn't bully me anymore, either." He looked at me. "Do you know how come?"

"A friend of mine made him stop."

"I need a friend like that," Jed said.

Chapter 21

Tuesday, October 31
Halloween

Back in California, Halloween had always been a pretty big deal. The neighborhood streets would be filled with children, and my father and I would go out trick-or-treating until he was tired of walking. This place was nothing like that. I didn't know if it was Utah or just my street, but only two kids came to our house. My mom was in bed and we didn't have any candy, so I gave them a jar of peaches. They took it.

I didn't have a costume, but it was so cold here I'd have to wear a coat over it anyway, so I found an old cowboy hat in the costume box. I hadn't walked Beau yet so I figured I could kill two birds with one stone. I took my bottle-collecting pillowcase and walked to Mr. Foster's and knocked on the door.

"It's Cowboy Richard," he said, opening the door. "You're supposed to say 'Trick or treat.' "

"I came to walk Beau."

"Very clever. Getting paid to trick-or-treat. Come in, I'll get the pooch."

I stepped inside. Mr. Foster fastened the leash on Beau, then led him over. "I'll have some hot cocoa waiting for you when you come back."

I stopped at every house up and down my street. Beau was his usual curious self, especially since we were walking into people's yards and there was more to sniff. I was glad for his company. Especially since the trick-or-treating went so poorly. There were only twelve homes on our street, and only five of them answered their door. One of them only opened to tell me that Halloween was of the devil. Another opened the door, looked at me, and shut it. They didn't say a thing. I guess I wasn't who they were expecting.

That's just the way this place was. The polygamist home didn't answer their door, though I saw one of the kids looking out between the drawn curtains at me.

I finished the street with just seven pieces of candy, and three of those came from Cliff at the Depot.

I suppose that I could have walked to another neighborhood, but the closest was several blocks away on the other side of the school, where Jed lived. He had told me horror stories about his neighborhood. He said that last year there were some teenagers who bullied the kids and took their candy. He said they stole a jack-o'-lantern from someone's porch, then smashed it on the street and made a kid eat it. I didn't want any of that.

I walked back to Mr. Foster's. This time I shouted, "Trick or treat!"

He opened the door. "Welcome back. How did the candy harvesting go?"

I showed him the seven candies in my bag. "Not good."

His brow furrowed. "Just a minute." He went over and got a bag of Brach's chocolate stars and dumped the entire bag into my sack. "That should help. I have your cocoa made. And I made some Halloween cookies."

There were sugar cookies in the shapes of pumpkins, bats, broomsticks, owls, and witches. They were covered with orange frosting.

I sat down at the table and lifted a witch.

"The lady at the pink house said that Halloween is of the devil."

"I suppose anything can be of the devil if you decide it is."

"Did you trick-or-treat when you were little?"

"Not like kids do today."

"In California everyone gave you candy." As I ate my cookie I noticed something I hadn't seen before. It looked like a wooden football. I walked over to it. "What is this?"

"It's called a washing bat and a battling block. My great-grandmother washed clothes with it on the plantation."

"Why didn't she just use a washing machine?"

"They didn't have those back then. She would put that block in a stream, then put the clothes on it and beat them clean with that bat. That's how slaves cleaned their clothes."

"Your great-grandmother was a slave?"

"Yes, she was."

Just then someone shouted, "Trick or treat!"

"Looks like we got someone." He took the plate of cookies over to the door and opened it. There were three children: Dracula, Frankenstein's monster, and a ghost, which was just a bedsheet with eye holes cut in it.

"Here you go," Mr. Foster said. "Take two if you like."

They each took a cookie, then ran back out to the street.

"You're welcome," Mr. Foster said as he shut the door. He offered me another cookie. This time I took an owl.

As I was eating he asked, "Do you have any friends?"

I finished what was in my mouth, then said, "I'm making a robot."

One of his eyebrows raised. "You're making a robot?"

I nodded. "His name is Tom. He can shock people."

"I'd like to meet this Tom. Maybe someday you could bring him over."

"He doesn't talk or anything yet."

He seemed to be pondering what I'd said. Then he asked, "Do you have any people friends?"

"I have you and Beau."

"Oh," he said softly. He slowly exhaled. "It's not easy moving to a new place, is it?"

Chapter 22

Saturday, November 11

Over the next ten days I fell into a routine of sorts. Every day I would stop at Mr. Foster's on the way home from school. It snowed four of the ten days, and between walking Beau and shoveling snow, I was getting rich. I figured that by the time Christmas was here I would have more than fifty dollars — way more than enough for Christmas presents. I remembered that it was Mr. Foster's birthday in December and I wanted to buy him something.

On Saturday, the eleventh, I noticed that Mr. Foster had hung an American flag next to his door. I climbed the stairs to his porch and rang the doorbell. As usual, Mr. Foster opened the door holding Beau. "Come in."

I took off my coat as I stepped inside. "How come you put up a flag?"

He set Beau down. "You don't know? It's Veterans Day."

"What's that?"
His brow fell. "You don't know Veterans Day? What do they teach you at that school?"
"Mostly fear," I said.
He grinned. "That's funny."
"Not to me." I sat down on the couch and Beau jumped on my lap and started licking my chin.
"Veterans Day is a national holiday to remember those who served in the military."
"You were in the army," I said. "Does that mean you're a veteran?"
"Yes. I hang the flag for my fellows who never came home. Like your brother."
I had never thought of my brother as a veteran. For that matter, I had never really thought of him as anything but gone.
"What did you do in the army?"
"I wasn't in the army. I was in the navy."
"You were on a ship?"
"The USS *Hornet.*"
"Did you ever kill anyone?"
He frowned. "That's not something you should ask a veteran."
"I'm sorry."
"Apology accepted. To answer your first question, I served in the mess."
"What's the mess?"
"The mess is what they called the navy

dining room."

"Is that because it was always a mess?"

He grinned. "No. We kept that place spick-and-span. *Mess* is an old French word that means a meal."

"What did you have to do?"

"I was what they called a culinary specialist. That's just a fancy military word for cook."

"Is that what you wanted to do?"

"No. That's what they told me to do. I wanted to be a gunner's mate. But it wasn't something they'd let me do."

"Because you were so good at cooking?"

"No, because I'm Black. At the start of the war, the US military wouldn't let Black people handle guns, so they put us in support roles, like cooking and truck repair and such."

"Why?"

"That's the sixty-four-thousand-dollar question. You would think that if any man offered to risk his life to defend his country, that that would be reason enough to let him. It wasn't until almost twenty thousand American men died at the Battle of the Bulge that they integrated Black soldiers with the white soldiers."

"Did it make you mad that they wouldn't let you do what you wanted to do?"

"It did at the time. But that was a long time ago. I never wanted to be someone who lived his whole life collecting all his injustices in a tin cup. Mr. Booker Washington said, 'We should not permit our grievances to overshadow our opportunities.'

"Everyone has problems — even white folk. The way I see it, a person's got two choices. One, he can hold on to his anger, or two, he can let his anger go. Only one of those choices brings freedom."

"I'm angry about the Vietnam War," I said.

"You've got every right to be angry. Just don't let your anger be you."

"What do you mean?"

"When I was young my mama told me this story. She said, 'There once was a man who hated the rain. Every time it rained, he would go outside and shake his fist and shout at the clouds. But, even with all his cussing and complaining, the rain wouldn't stop. He'd shout and shout until he'd finally give up. Then he'd go back inside. He was still angry, but now he'd be hoarse and shivering. After a while, everyone around him got sick and tired of hearing him cuss and left him.

" 'One day he was out shouting so long that he caught the influenza, and since no one was with him anymore, he died all alone. That was the end of him. And you know what? At his funeral, when they went to bury him, it rained.' "

"That's a sad story," I said.

He nodded. "Sad for him." He walked back to the kitchen. "I've got to finish cooking this custard. You can go ahead and take Beau out. His leash is on the floor over by the phonograph."

I took Beau for his usual walk of about a mile. When I got back to the house, I rubbed his feet with a dry rag, then set him on the floor.

"You're just in time," Mr. Foster said. "My custard cake is done, and it is delicious. Sit and have a piece."

I sat down at the table and Mr. Foster set a piece of the cake in front of me. It was a light sponge cake with a creamy custard center, its top sprinkled with powdered sugar.

Mr. Foster sat down across from me with his own piece. "Since you left with Beau, you got me thinking about what we talked about — about holding on to anger. I had this thought. Do you know what alchemy is?"

"Is it like chemistry?"

"You could say that. Long ago people thought they could turn lead into gold. They called that alchemy. The idea behind alchemy was to take something worthless and turn it into something of value." He looked at me intently. "Forgiveness is alchemy. To take something so base and ugly that you don't even want to think of it and turn it into something noble and fine. That is true alchemy. Remember that. It's not always easy, but if you can do that, you'll have a happy life.

"I want to show you something." He walked over to his curio cabinet in the corner and took out a small jade-green vase, then brought it over to the table. It was beautiful, with jagged veins of gold running through it.

"After the war, a friend of mine gave this to me. His name was Jim, and he was a soldier from Alabama I met on the *Hornet.* Before the war was over, we were stationed outside Okinawa. Jim was integrated into a fighting squad. He saw some of the fiercest fighting of the entire war. This vase was a souvenir he brought back from Japan. It's called Kintsugi."

He pointed at the veins of gold. "These jagged lines are where the vase was once broken. The Japanese believed that just because something had been broken didn't make it any less valuable. In fact, they believed the opposite was true. They would carefully repair the vase with a special tree sap, then, after it had cured, they would paint the mends with gold. The result is this beautiful design."

I reached out and touched the vase. "Is that real gold?"

He nodded. "Yes. You see, this vase is worth much more now than it was before it was shattered."

"I dropped a vase once," I said. "But I just got in trouble."

"There's an important lesson here, but maybe you won't understand it until you're a little older." He returned the vase to the cabinet, locked it, then turned back to me. "It's getting late. You should be on your way home. I'll give you some cake to take home for your mama."

He walked to the kitchen and put four large pieces of the cake on a plate. As I was about to leave he said, "Thanksgiving is the week after next. Do you know what you and your mama are doing?"

I shook my head. "She hasn't said anything about it."

"Would you ask your mama if the two of you, and your papa, would like to join Beau and me for Thanksgiving dinner? I'm in the mood to cook up something special, and it's been too long since I really did it up right."

"I'll ask her."

"You do that. Then let me know what she says so I can prepare. Good night, King Richard."

"Good night."

I walked home carrying the plate of cake before me. I hoped my mother would let us celebrate Thanksgiving with Mr. Foster.

Chapter 23

Thursday, November 23
Thanksgiving

My mother told me to tell Mr. Foster that we would be happy to join him for Thanksgiving dinner. At first, my father even said he would come, but he changed his mind two days before, saying that with the holiday rush he had to work. Maybe he was telling the truth, but I kind of thought that with the way things were with my mother, he didn't want to eat dinner at a stranger's house.

My mother went out the day before Thanksgiving to buy flowers and ingredients for a pumpkin pie, which she was making when I got home from walking Beau. I was glad to see her out of her bedroom.

It had snowed the night before and I spent most of the afternoon shoveling snow. I was getting better at it, because I was able to do both driveways without stopping to rest. I would have done Mr. Foster's for free anyway, but the three dollars he paid me was a great motivator, too.

A little before two o'clock my mother and I gathered up the pie and flowers and walked over to Mr. Foster's house.

"You did a good job on our driveways," my mother said as we crossed from our yard into his.

"It's no big deal," I said, even though it was.

We knocked on Mr. Foster's door, which always elicited a manic response from Beau. Mr. Foster answered the door wearing an apron.

"Welcome, neighbors. Happy Thanksgiving."

"Happy Thanksgiving to you," my mother said back. She held out the bouquet. "These are for you."

"Thank you very much. I don't remember the last time someone brought me flowers."

"We brought a pumpkin pie," I said.

"Even better. I love me some pumpkin pie. Come in, please, come in. Richard, you can set the pie on the counter next to the apple pie."

The pie he'd made had a latticed top sprinkled with sugar. Everything Mr. Foster baked looked like it would win a blue ribbon.

Beau, of course, was at my feet. He had been given a bath for the day and his hair was shiny and fluffy. I set the pie down, then crouched down to scratch his belly. "Hey, Beau. Happy Thanksgiving."

"He's thankful for you," Mr. Foster said. He turned to my mother. "I'm afraid he loves Richard more than he loves me. I get feeling a little jealous sometimes."

"I'm sure that's not true," she said.

"Don't be too sure," he said.

My mother looked around the room. "Your home is lovely."

"Thank you."

In anticipation of guests, Mr. Foster had tidied things up and the home smelled even more aromatic than usual. On top of the console was a scented candle with a holly leaf crown at its base. A Burl Ives Christmas album was playing.

There was a crackling fire in the fireplace and the table was set with fine dinnerware. Mr. Foster put the flowers in a glass vase, then brought them over to the table for a centerpiece.

My mother lifted a dinner plate to examine it. "You have lovely china. Is this Currier and Ives?"

Lovely was a word my mother used a lot when she was complimenting something.

"Yes, young lady, and thank you."

"Please, call me June."

"June was my great-aunt's name." He walked back to the kitchen. "I don't know why it is, but it seems that food always tastes better when it's served on fine dinnerware."

"Maybe that's why we put beautiful paintings in frames," my mother said.

Mr. Foster smiled. "I believe you're right."

The turkey, which rested on a porcelain platter, was beautifully glazed and larger than the one we usually got. The whole table looked like something out of one of my mother's lady magazines. Mr. Foster even had a plate on the ground for Beau, who was acting a little more subdued than usual.

"I'm just finishing up a few last things. Please, sit down."

"Can I help?" my mother asked.

"No, no, I've got everything under control." He smiled. "Famous last words." The tinny bell of the oven timer began to ring. "And there are the rolls. *La meilleure partie.*" He pulled a tray from the oven. "I like to wait until just before dinner to bring out the rolls. There's nothing like a hot-from-the-oven buttered roll." He set the pan of rolls on the counter. "We'll let them settle for a moment."

"Where would you like us to sit?" my mother asked.

"Wherever you like."

My mother and I sat down opposite each other, leaving the head of the table for Mr. Foster.

"There's certainly a lot of food," my mother said.

"I figure if I'm going to go to the trouble of making something special, I should be cooking for a few meals. Some things taste even better the second time around. Especially the turkey. You've got turkey sandwiches, turkey soup, turkey salad, turkey and dumplings. Not to mention Beau loves it."

"You feed Beau turkey?" I asked.

"He would hold it against me if I didn't."

My mother watched him flip the rolls from the pan into a basket. "Are those Parker House rolls?"

"Yes, they are."

"I grew up with those. They were my mother's specialty."

"I know," he said, bringing the basket over to the table. "These are your mama's rolls." He broke them apart and put one on each of our plates.

"I can't believe my mother shared her

recipe with you. She said it was going to die with her. It almost did. I got it out of her at a moment of weakness."

He smiled. "Mrs. Esther was as protective of her recipes as a mama is with a newborn child. I'm grateful for it. I had to trade her a recipe she wanted as much as I wanted hers. Fortunately, I had a corn bread recipe she wanted."

He walked over and turned down the phonograph, then sat down at the head of the table. "If you don't mind, I'd like to offer a Thanksgiving prayer."

"We'd like that," my mother said. Taking our cue from Mr. Foster, we all bowed our heads.

"Dear Lord, we are indeed grateful this day for the abundance of our lives. Help us to remember that you are the giver of all blessings. Thank you for this delicious food and for good neighbors to share it with. Beau and I are grateful to have new friends and we pray, dear Lord, that your favor will shine upon them like the morning sun. Amen."

"Amen," we echoed.

"Thank you," my mother added.

When Mr. Foster said he wanted to cook up something special, he wasn't exaggerating. At our usual Thanksgiving dinner we had the traditional fare: turkey, stuffing, rolls, mashed potatoes, and candied yams. Mr. Foster had all those things and more, including a few things I'd never seen before: deviled eggs, corn soufflé, collard greens, and corn bread. I felt sorry that my father had to miss it. He would have really liked it.

"A lot of the food is what my mama made. There is nothing like southern cooking to a southern boy."

"It all looks delicious," my mother said. "Thank you for thinking of us. It's a treat to have Thanksgiving with a chef."

"Who told you I was a chef?"

"My mother told me a long time ago. But I can tell just by looking at your food that you're a culinary artist."

"Culinary artist," he repeated. "I like that. Thank you. That is the most generous compliment I've received in a long time. Do you know you look like your mama?"

My mother smiled. "That is the kindest compliment *I've* received in a long time."

"I meant it as a compliment. Your mama was a lovely woman and a good neighbor. She's the only one in the neighborhood who ever visited me."

"Certainly your neighbors' loss," my mother said. "Speaking of visits, I hope Ricky isn't bothering you too much."

He glanced over at me. "Bothering? Richard's visits are the best part of Beau's and my day. I can't get out like I used to, so I'm grateful for his company. He's also been such a big help, walking Beau and shoveling the snow. I don't know what I'd do without him."

Hearing that made me happy.

Mr. Foster lifted Beau's plate from the floor, put some turkey and stuffing on it, then set it back down. Beau gulped it down.

"I told you, Beau loves that turkey. He'd eat himself sick if I let him. He likes the giblet gravy, too, but he makes too big a mess of it. And he likes the corn bread, with just a touch of honey."

"I hear you used to own a bakery," my mother said.

"I did long ago. I had a little bakery in Huntsville, Alabama."

"He baked things for the governor of Alabama," I said.

"I'm not surprised," my mother said. "Where did you learn to cook?"

"Well, first at my mama's side. She was a magician with food. She used to make corn bread and I'd walk up and down the street and sell it. I always sold all she made.

"Then, when I joined the navy, they put me in the kitchen. With the food rationing and all, I taught myself tricks to make it better for the men. You never knew when it might be their last meal."

"Where did you serve in the navy?"

"I was in the Pacific Fleet. I served on the USS *Hornet* under the command of Captain Marshall White. I was in the Battle of Midway. We always served the men something special if we knew it would be a hard day. That morning we served steak and eggs for breakfast. We sent out our torpedo bombers that day, but only one of our aviators came back."

"That's horrible," my mother said.

"Those men were heroes. It was an honor to feed them."

The meal was long and pleasant. I had three helpings, which seemed to please Mr. Foster. "Richard has a hollow leg," he said happily.

After we finished eating, Mr. Foster put the pies on the table, then he brought over a cup of coffee for my mother and a cup of cocoa for me. I still considered his packaged cocoa a miracle of the modern age.

"Mr. Foster has cocoa that doesn't need milk," I said. "It comes in an envelope."

"Does it taste the same?" she asked.

"Better," I said.

"It's called Swiss Miss," Mr. Foster said.

"It already has powdered milk in it, so I just add hot water."

"That's very clever." She took a sip of her coffee, then said, "Do you have plans for Christmas?"

"A lot of baking," he said.

"And he's going to see his family," I said.

"That sounds nice. How long has it been since you've seen them?"

"Too long for my liking. Much too long."

"How long will you be with them?"

"I suppose that depends on how long they'll tolerate me," he said. He turned to me. "I don't think I'll be able to bring Beau with me. Do you think you could help me by watching him while I'm gone?"

I turned to my mother. "Can I?"

"Of course," she said.

"That's a big worry off my mind," he said.

I was thrilled. I always wanted to bring Beau home. It would be just like having my own dog.

"What are your Christmas plans?" Mr. Foster asked.

My mother's smile fell. "This year has been difficult, so I honestly haven't given it much thought. We haven't got a Christmas tree yet. I don't even know where we put the decorations."

"They're in the back room," I said. "Next

to the piano." I knew exactly where they were. I had opened the boxes weeks earlier, hoping to get them out.

"Richard has told me a little about your year," Mr. Foster said. "I'm so sorry for your losses."

"Thank you," my mother said softly. "It's been a hard year."

He just looked at her kindly, then said, "May I get you another piece of pie?"

With the exception of my father's absence, it was one of the best Thanksgivings of my life. Mr. Foster wouldn't even let us help with the dishes.

out. I wondered if other kids' mothers stayed in their bedrooms most of the time or if it was just the ones with no fathers.

Fortunately, Mr. Foster's home was filled with enough Christmas for both our houses. During one of my visits, he brought out an old train and I helped him lay its tracks around his tree. The train wasn't like the mass-produced plastic ones that ran on batteries and were decorated with cheap decals. This one was heavy, forged from cast metal, and hand-painted. It ran from an electric box with a large black dial you could turn to control the train's speed.

The thing drove Beau crazy, and he chased it around the tree, yapping and nipping at it until either he derailed it or Mr. Foster turned it off to get some peace.

"I keep thinking he'll get used to it," Mr. Foster said. "But I don't think he ever will. He just wants to *give it the business.*"

"He likes to chase things," I said.

He grinned. "Me too," he said dryly. "A long, long time ago."

I had no idea what he meant.

One day he asked, "What are you asking Santa Claus for Christmas?"

I had a ready answer. "A GI Joe navy scuba set, with a real raft you can blow up, and a chemistry set. They have one that you can take fingerprints, so if someone burglarizes your house, you can catch them."

"Those both sound like excellent toys," he said.

They really were. Back then chemistry sets were much more exciting. They came with chemicals that could explode or catch fire. The world was much more adventurous back then.

"What do you want for Christmas?" I asked.

"I haven't given it much thought," he said. "Beau always forgets to give me something. Let me think about it." He pondered for a moment, then said, "I would like a necktie."

"A necktie?"

"A men's necktie made from real silk. Maybe a navy blue one with gold stripes, diagonal like this." He moved his hand in a diagonal motion across his chest. "I've never had much use for a necktie. I suppose I still don't. But I'd hate to go through life and never have a necktie."

"That's not asking very much," I said. "Santa will bring you one if you ask."

"I hope he will." He smiled. "Because I know Beau won't."

That's pretty much how things went that first week of December. I would come home from school, walk Beau, then go inside Mr.

Foster's house for a cocoa and the baking of the day. That was always the best part of my day. Sometimes it was the only good part of my day.

My father didn't come home. We talked once on the telephone, but it was only because he called to talk to my mom and I answered. He apologized and said he was very busy at work, which made it even less likely that he would be coming back home before Christmas.

Except for Mr. Foster and Beau, my Christmas season was off to an uneventful beginning. In fact, nothing much happened until the Friday afternoon when Mrs. Covey dropped a bomb that would change all of our lives. It was a day to live in infamy.

CHAPTER 25

Friday, December 8

It was Friday afternoon, mere minutes until freedom. We kids were working silently at our desks, waiting for the bell to release us, when Mrs. Covey rose from her desk. She walked to the blackboard and clapped her hands to get our attention.

"Put away your work," she said.

We quickly obeyed. After we had settled, she said, "Christmas is coming." The way she said it you'd think she was warning us of an impending disaster. Mrs. Covey had a gift for making things sound terrible. Even Christmas.

She looked around the room. "Are you excited for Christmas? If you're excited for Christmas, raise your hand."

All hands rose.

"Are you excited for Santa Claus to come down that chimney, bringing you lots of toys?"

We all raised our hands again. I was astonished that the Christmas spirit had even pierced Mrs. Covey's ornery shell.

"Have any of you ever climbed down a chimney? Raise your hand if you've climbed down a chimney."

One hand rose. It was Benjamin Hardy, a sandy-haired kid who was usually pretty quiet.

"Mr. Hardy, you've been down a chimney?"

"I got on the roof and looked down one once."

"That's not what I asked. Put your hand down."

Benjamin lowered his hand.

"Chimneys weren't designed for human passage. Except for Tami, you're all pretty small . . ."

Everyone looked at Tami. She turned bright red.

". . . But even as small as you are, you would all still get stuck in a chimney. Just think how big Santa is, not to mention his bag of toys."

"Santa's bigger than Tami," Dwight said. I think he was trying to be nice, but Tami still looked miserable.

"Yes, he is. So how is it that Santa manages to fit down a chimney?"

Another hand went up.

"Yes, Patty?"

"Magic."

"You're telling us that Santa uses magic?"

"Yes, ma'am."

"So, Santa magically slides down the chimney." She walked to her desk. "If Santa's so magical, why doesn't he just poof the presents into the house? Or, for that matter, poof all the presents into all the houses in the world at the same time?" Patty didn't answer. Mrs. Covey looked around the room. "Anyone?"

The bell rang. Not that it mattered. In Mrs. Covey's class, like in professional boxing, there was no being saved by the bell. No one stood, except Patty.

"Where do you think you're going?"

"The bell rang."

"Did you hear me say that you were dismissed?"

"No, ma'am."

"Then plant your bottom back in your chair. I'm not done."

Patty quickly sat back down.

Mrs. Covey slowly gazed around the room. "Let me tell you something, people. Santa doesn't come down the chimney. He doesn't fly around two hundred million surface miles of the earth just to fill a stocking you hung by your chimney. He doesn't have flying reindeer. Reindeer can't fly any more than I can.

"How do I know this? Because, children, there is no Santa Claus. There are no flying reindeer; there are no magic elves making toys packaged in Mattel toy boxes. It's all a myth and you're too old to believe such nonsense. Don't be so stupid."

Her words shook us to the core. After a moment, one of the boys raised his hand.

"What, Nick?"

"My mom said that Santa is real."

Mrs. Covey slowly shook her head. "Your mother lied to you. Wake up, children. If your parents told you that there is a Santa Claus, your parents are liars. There is no Santa Claus. There is no such thing as magic." She looked around the room as the weight of her words crushed us. "All right. You're dismissed."

The impact of her words was palpable. For a moment no one moved. Then, one by one, we rose, shuffling out of the classroom, as if we had all just learned of the death of a dear friend. In a way I suppose that was exactly what had happened.

I walked home feeling like my heart was in a vise and my mind was wandering through a labyrinth of confusion and loss. I thought of stopping at Mr. Foster's, but I was too upset. I went straight to my bedroom and laid on my bed.

Several hours later I knocked on my mother's door.

"Mom."

"Yes, honey?"

I opened her door. As usual the room was dark and my mother was lying in the center of her bed with a cold pack on her forehead.

"How was school?" she asked softly.

I walked to her side, waiting for my eyes to adjust to the darkness. I needed to see her face when I asked the question.

"Is Santa Claus real?"

"Of course he is, honey."

I swallowed. "Mrs. Covey said that there is no Santa Claus. And that you were lying to us."

My mother hesitated. "Santa Claus is the spirit of giving."

"But he lives at the North Pole. And he has reindeer and a sleigh, and he comes down the chimney . . ."

My mother looked at me sadly, then slowly sighed. "No, honey. There is no Santa Claus."

My chest froze. I couldn't believe that Mrs. Covey was right. What other horribleness had she been right about? I thought

for a moment, then said, “Mom?”
“Yes, honey?”
“Did you lie about Jesus, too?”

CHAPTER 26

I believe that it was at that moment when I came to the terrifying realization that there was nothing in my life that couldn't be taken away. My father was gone. My brother was gone. Our house was gone. The whole state of California was gone. Now even Santa Claus had deserted me. There was not a single thing I could hold on to. I wondered how long my mother would last. I had never felt so scared in all my life.

That night I dreamed of a lavishly decorated Christmas tree. It was exquisite — sparkling with gold and silver tinsel, with an alabaster angel on top. I realized that the angel was alive. She turned to look at me, and her wings spread open like a great book.

At the base of the tree was a mountain of presents wrapped in elegant paper and silk bows. The tree was strung with shimmering lights that lit the room in a brilliant and growing illumination.

Suddenly I realized that the radiance wasn't coming from the tree's lights. The tree was on fire. The blaze grew quickly. It consumed the tree and the presents, then spread to the rest of the house. I fled outside, but no one else in my family was there.

When the fire was done, I was all alone. There was nothing left but a mountain of ash and the smoking remains of what had once been Christmas.

CHAPTER 27

The next morning felt colder than usual. It was a Saturday morning, usually my happiest day of the week, but you wouldn't know it. My heart ached. I didn't even watch cartoons.

Around ten I walked over and knocked on Mr. Foster's door. I heard his slow shuffle to the door as Beau barked excitedly.

"King Richard. Come in. Are you here to take Beau on his walk?"

"I need to tell you something."

He must have sensed the gravity of my mood as his expression changed to one of concern. "Have a seat at the table. I made cookies yesterday." As I sat down he said, "You didn't come by yesterday afternoon."

"I had to talk to my mom."

"Did something bad happen?"

"Yes." I was suddenly embarrassed to tell him. I felt stupid for believing for so long.

He sat down across from me at the table

with a plate of chocolate chip cookies. I didn't take one.

"Go on," he said.

"Mrs. Covey told us that there isn't a Santa Claus. She said there's no such thing as magic." My voice cracked. "She said my parents are liars."

Mr. Foster just looked at me, his expression growing even more serious. "That must have been awful painful to hear."

"It was."

"Especially from such a cruel lady."

I furtively wiped a tear from my cheek, which he kindly pretended not to notice. When I could speak, I asked, "How did you know she was cruel?"

"Only a cruel person would steal someone's happiness like that." He leaned forward. "Let me tell you something, Richard. Something I want you to always remember.

"This won't be the only time in your life that someone tries to steal your dreams. There are Mrs. Coveys all over this world. They are young and old, male and female, Black and white. They are people who are too unhappy and too cowardly to believe in their own dreams, so they justify their misery by throwing stones at other people's dreams." He looked at me for a moment, then stood. "I'll make you a hot cocoa.

There's almost nothing in the world that a hot cocoa can't make better."

He put the teapot on the stove, then said, "You stay there. I want to show you something." He left the room. A few minutes later he walked back into the kitchen. To my surprise he was wearing a Santa Claus suit.

"I disagree with your teacher. There is magic in this world. And if I can be Santa, there must be a Santa Claus."

"You can't be Santa," I said.

"Why not?"

"Because . . . you're . . ."

"Black?"

I nodded.

"A Black man can't be Santa Claus?"

"No."

"Why not?"

"He's not Black in the pictures."

Mr. Foster just looked at me. "Pictures? Are you telling me that you've got photographic pictures of the actual Santa Claus? Real black-and-white — no, sorry, just white-and-white, pictures of the old man?"

"There are pictures in my mom's magazines."

"Then, what you mean is, you've seen a Coca-Cola advertisement with a jolly old white man." He shook his head. "You think

Black children want a fat white man to come down their chimney? That would terrify them."

I had never thought of it that way.

"Santa is the spirit of giving, and spirits don't have colors. They're like . . . water."

As if on cue, the teakettle started whistling. He walked over to it, poured the steaming water into a mug, mixed it with his Swiss Miss, then set it down on the table. He sat down across from me.

"Let me tell you something, Richard. Something I've dealt with my entire life. What you said about Santa Claus not being Black — it's just like those pictures of Jesus you see in white-people churches. Jesus looks like he came from Iowa, not Jerusalem. Jesus wasn't American. He wasn't even white. Jesus was from the Middle East. Have you ever seen people from the Middle East? They're not white. But that's the way they go painting him, like some Gary Cooper, Hollywood movie star actor." He leaned back in his chair. "I know why they do it. People want people to look like themselves. It makes them feel safer."

I didn't know what to say. After a minute I asked, "Why do you have a Santa Claus suit?"

"I used to be a bell ringer for the Salvation Army."

"What's a bell ringer?"

"Bell ringers stand in front of grocery stores and ring a bell so people put money in the bucket to help the poor."

"Do you still do that?"

"No. The cold gets to me now. But I did like doing that. I got to see people be a little better version of themselves. Not always, but a lot of them."

I took a drink of the cocoa. "I'm sorry I said you couldn't be Santa."

"Apology accepted."

"I wish you really were Santa."

"Why is that?"

"Because I could believe in you."

To my surprise his eyes welled up. He walked around the table in his red suit and hugged me. "I believe in you, too, Richard. Never forget that. I believe in you, too."

CHAPTER 28

On Sunday afternoon, I had just come in from building a snow fort to find my mother in the kitchen. She had made me a grilled cheese sandwich with bean and bacon soup.

"Your father is taking you out next Tuesday night."

"Did he call?"

She nodded. I wished I had answered the phone. I wanted to talk to him. I missed him. My mother sat down at the table, putting her head in her hands.

"Do you have a headache?" I asked.

"I always do."

"Maybe it's because we live in Utah. Maybe we should all just go back to California and start all over."

She raised her head to look at me, then, without a word, got up and walked back to her room.

Chapter 29

It was Tuesday night. The night my father was coming for me. I had just taken Beau on his walk, put the dollar Mr. Foster gave me in my safe, then took out two five-dollar bills. "Lincolns," Cliff at the Depot called them. I wanted to show them to my father. I wanted to impress him.

I had noticed that my mother had been especially quiet that day and her eyes were puffy. She didn't say a thing about me going out with my father. I went to ask her if she wanted me to make her something for dinner, but when I was outside her door I could hear her crying. It made me feel sick inside. I sat on the floor outside her door for more than five minutes before she stopped crying. I never knocked. I wouldn't know what to say anyway.

My father arrived about twenty minutes after six o'clock. He was late, but I was just glad he showed up. He was wearing a blue jacket with the words *Sears and Roebuck* embroidered on the left breast. I wanted to tell my father about my mother, but he acted like he didn't want to see her. He didn't even walk past the front room.

"Get your coat," he said. When we were in his car he asked, "How does Shakey's Pizza sound?"

"There's a Shakey's Pizza Parlor here?"

"Just like in California."

This was good news. First my father was here, now Shakey's.

"I love Shakey's."

"Shakey's it is."

As my father backed his car out of the driveway he asked, "Did you shovel the driveway?"

"Yes."

"That's the entrepreneurial spirit. When I was your age, I would walk up and down my street and shovel walks for money."

"I tried that. I only got a nickel."

"Someone gave you a nickel for shoveling their walk?"

"Yes. And it was a long driveway. It took me two hours."

"Cheapskate," he said. "Never go back there."

He didn't have to tell me that.

Shakey's Pizza wasn't very far from our

home, though I'm not surprised that I'd never seen it. My mother and I never got out much.

Walking into the pizza parlor was like walking into a time machine — the employees in their familiar straw hats and red-striped shirts, the player piano belting out ragtime music, and the oregano smell of baking pizzas brought back pleasant memories of our outings in California. The hostess sat us down at a table with a red-and-white checkered tablecloth and handed us menus.

"Do you know what you want?" my father asked.

"Pizza."

"Well, I figured that. What kind of pizza?"

"I want the Big Ed Special."

"What do you know? I was thinking of getting the Big Ed Special, too. How about we order a large Big Ed and share. And we should also get us some of those mojo potatoes."

I looked down at the paper menu. A large Big Ed Special pizza was $2.10. Mojo potatoes were just forty-five cents.

"I can pay for it," I said. I reached into my pocket and brought out a five-dollar bill. My father looked as surprised as I hoped he would.

"Where did you get that kind of money?"

"I've been collecting bottles for refunds. Mr. Foster had a whole bunch of them."

"Mr. Foster, the man next door?"

I nodded. "He also pays me to walk his dog, Beau, every day. Except Sunday. That's Beau's day of rest."

"A dog's whole life is a day of rest," he said.

"Mr. Foster said that the Bible says that Sunday is to be a day of rest for animals."

He lightly smiled. "I just hope he pays you more than a nickel."

I put the bill back in my pocket. "He pays me a dollar."

"Whoa. Maybe you should be buying our pizza."

After the waitress took our order, my father asked, "How is school?"

I frowned. "I hate it. My teacher's a troll."

"I'm sorry."

"Mrs. Covey told us that there is no Santa Claus. And she called you and Mom liars."

"She called us liars?"

"Yes."

"Maybe I need to have a talk with Mrs. Covey. What did your mom say?"

"She said Santa wasn't real."

"I'm sorry you had to hear it that way. Santa is the spirit of giving."

"Everyone says that," I said. "But only after you find out he isn't real."

"You're right," he said. "You're right."

We sat a moment in silence, then I asked, "What's your job?"

"I'm delivering appliances for Sears and Roebuck."

"In your car?"

"No. Big things like washers and driers, dishwashers. The Kenmore line. We drive a truck."

"Do you like doing that?"

"Not particularly. But a man's got to work. I'm just doing it until I can get back to what I used to do."

The waitress brought us our food. After I had downed a couple of slices of pizza, I said, "Mom said the people in Utah were nice, but they're not. She lied."

"She didn't lie. It's just how she remembers it. When she was little, this part of Salt Lake City was rural."

"What's rural?"

"Rural means like in the country, or farmland. Her parents had chickens and milking cows. That field just south of the house used to be a cornfield. Country people are simpler than city folk. But they've either gotten old or moved out. Now this area is considered inner city, so you have bars and pawnshops. That attracts a different kind of people."

"Mean people?"

"Maybe less-happy people."

"Like Mrs. Covey?"

He nodded. "Sounds like Mrs. Covey."

We went back to eating in silence. After a few minutes I blurted out what I had been wanting to ask since he'd picked me up. "Are you going to come home for Christmas?"

He stopped eating. "Your mother and I still haven't worked things out."

His answer hurt but I held back from showing my feelings.

"I miss our family," I said.

My father was quiet a moment, then said, "I miss it, too, son."

"Then why don't you just come home?"

He didn't answer. The silence grew painful, and I was glad when a banjo player started plucking a happy tune.

Finally my father said, "I wish it were that easy."

Maybe it was desperation talking, but I felt unusually bold. "It *is* really easy," I said. "Just come home and don't leave."

He breathed out slowly. "Things get more complicated when you're older. Since Mark died, it hasn't been the same."

anyone else until I saw Mr. Foster. He was sitting on a chair, leaning forward on his cane. I had never really seen him out of his house, so he looked out of place in this crowd of people. I went to him.

"Why is everyone here? Where's my mom?"

He looked sad. "Richard, your mama tried to take her life."

My heart froze. "Is she still alive?"

"Yes. Help got here in time."

Just then I heard shouting. I looked over to see what was going on. My oldest aunt, Wilda — the matriarch of the family — was standing in front of the bedroom door, barring my father from entering.

"Get out of my way," he said. "This is my house."

"No, it's not."

"She's my wife."

"You could have fooled me," Aunt Wilda said sharply.

The man next to her, probably my uncle, was a tall, burly man, with thick arms and a full beard. He was at least half a head taller than my father. He stepped in front of my dad, the two men looking threateningly into each other's eyes.

Just as the situation looked like it might erupt into something even more terrible, one of the ambulance attendants shouted at them to move as they brought my mother out of her room on a gurney. I ran to her side.

"Mom."

She opened her eyes and looked up at me but didn't say anything. I looked over to my father. He looked as helpless as I felt. I followed her out to the ambulance. The men lifted the gurney into the back, then shut the door as I blinked back my tears. I was gulping and ticcing.

Mr. Foster walked up behind me and put his hand on my shoulder. "She'll be okay," he said. "I'll pray for her." As the ambulance backed out of our driveway he looked over at my father, who had been standing next to it. "You need to be with your papa."

I just sniffed.

He walked over to my father and said something, then he patted my father on the arm, turned, and hobbled back to his house. He was moving slower than usual.

As the crowd dissipated, I walked over to my father. He put his arm around me. Neither of us knew what to say.

Chapter 31

I didn't go to school for the rest of the week. There was talk of sending me to stay with one of the aunts, but I told my father that I would rather live in the chicken coop. He told everyone that I was his son and that he would be staying here with me.

Neither my father nor I was much on cooking, so almost every night we ate out, which, back then, was a rare treat. We went to McDonald's, Arctic Circle, and a new taco place called Taco Time. I loved going out but especially spending the time with my father. I was just glad to finally have him back home. Like it used to be.

While my father was at work, I stayed inside and read. I finished *The Hobbit* and started the Hardy Boys — a series about two teenage brothers who were amateur detectives and solved all sorts of crimes, from diamond smuggling to racehorse kidnapping. It was good adventure, and more and more I discovered the power of losing myself in books. It was the only time I didn't fret about my mother.

I didn't go out to the garage to work on my robot. I guess I had finally abandoned him for good, leaving him to be infested by mice on the garage floor.

More than anything I wanted to see my mother. Thursday, I asked my father if we could go see her. He called the hospital, but they said she wasn't allowed visitors. When he asked how long she would be there, no one seemed to have an answer.

It snowed off and on for the rest of the week. Twice a day I went out and shoveled our driveway so it wouldn't get too deep for me to handle. I did the same for Mr. Foster's driveway as well.

Thursday, when I went up to Mr. Foster's door to tell him that I had finished shoveling his driveway, he acted different than usual. It was the very first time that he didn't invite me in. He also said that Beau wouldn't be needing a walk. I went home feeling very sad. Even the Hardy Boys couldn't take my mind from my sadness.

It snowed that night, so Friday morning I went over to shovel Mr. Foster's driveway, but he wasn't even home. I could see his car's tire tracks in the snow. Up to then I had never seen him leave his house, though he could have when I was at school.

It was late afternoon when he finally returned. I went up to his door to get Beau, but he didn't answer, which only hurt my heart more. I wondered if I had said something wrong, like I had when my mother slapped me.

Later that afternoon the young Black woman I'd seen a few weeks earlier came over again. I was out in my driveway when she pulled up in front of his house. This time she waved to me. I didn't wave back. I didn't like her. I wondered who she was and why she got to go inside, and I didn't. Maybe she was his new friend. Most of all, I wondered why Mr. Foster didn't want to see me when I needed him the most.

All the while, the Christmas season was gaining on us. It was less than ten days until Christmas, and four days until Mr. Foster's birthday.

Earlier in the week I had asked my father if he would take me Christmas shopping on Saturday, since that was his day off. He promised he would.

Saturday morning, I poured myself a bowl of cereal, then took it in the front room to watch cartoons while I waited for my father to get up. During the final minutes of

George of the Jungle, the phone rang. I ran for it, hoping it was my mother.

"Hello."

An older woman asked, "Is this the Evans residence?"

"Yes, ma'am."

"Is your father home?"

"Just a moment." I knocked on his bedroom door. "Dad, someone's on the phone for you."

"Thank you," he said back through the closed door. I heard a muffled "Hello." I walked away wondering who it was.

About a cartoon later my father walked into the front room. He was showered and dressed.

"All right, sport," he said. "Have you had your breakfast?"

"I had cereal."

"Great. I'm just going to grab a coffee and toast and then we'll be on our way."

A couple of minutes later he walked out of the kitchen carrying a coffee mug and a piece of buttered toast with a bite out of it. "This is good bread. Did your mom make it?"

"Mr. Foster made it."

"Maybe we should have been eating over there." He settled into a chair. "So where would you like to go Christmas shopping?"

"Can we go to the Cottonwood Mall?"

He grimaced. "You know it's going to be the busiest shopping day of the year. The mall crowds are going to be insane."

"I don't care," I said.

"All right. Get your coat and let's go."

"Wait," I said. "I need to get my money." I ran to my room and took twenty dollars out of my safe. I really felt rich.

The Cottonwood Mall was about ten minutes from our home. It was Utah's first enclosed mall and had opened just five years earlier. It was, as my father predicted, insanely crowded. We parked in one of the few remaining spaces at the south end of the mall and walked in through the JCPenney entrance, which is where I wanted to go.

My father said he had some shopping of his own, so we agreed to meet up in one hour at the pet store near JCPenney. Fortunately, I had my Mickey Mouse watch.

I had already decided what I was getting everyone for Christmas. I was buying two neckties, one for my father and the other for Mr. Foster.

In the mid-sixties, necktie fashion ran the gamut from traditional apron ties to silk ascots and cravats to skinny, flat-ended ties. I asked a salesclerk to help me pick out my ties. He asked me who the ties were for. After I told him he said, "Sounds like we want to stay a little more conservative. Wide ties are on their way back. I have something just right for the mature gents."

The price of silk ties ranged from 97¢ to $1.47. I bought my father a dark brown tie with rust and gold stripes. My mother had a dress nearly that same color, so I thought they would look good together. I got Mr. Foster what he had suggested when he told me that he wanted a necktie — a navy blue silk tie with gold diagonal stripes.

After the clerk had wrapped up my ties, I went over to the women's department, where I bought my mother a purple scarf with pink and gold geometric patterns and Vivara Parfum — a foreign-sounding perfume that the lady at the counter recommended. "Vivara Parfum, your girl will swoon," she sang. I don't know if she made that up or if it was their slogan.

I just had Beau to shop for. My favorite store in the mall was the pet shop — the same one I'd walked through back in October when I went school-clothes shopping with my mother.

Even though I went there to get something for Beau, I ended up spending almost all my time just looking at the animals. The place echoed with the sound of barking. They had a whole wall of kennels with all sorts of dogs, though, I thought, none as cute as Beau.

There were other mammals, like white mice and guinea pigs and hamsters in metal cages with spinning wheels. I wondered if I could sell them some of the mice in our house, since my bottle deposit income had drastically declined because it was nearly impossible to find bottles in the snow. Considering how many mice we had around our place, I could be a millionaire.

But the real draw for me was the exotic animals. They had a bright green iguana, a baby alligator with yellow eyes, a three-foot-long boa constrictor, and an entire wall covered with aquariums, with a wide assortment of exotic fish, including blind cave fish and ghost catfish — a transparent fish you could see through. (You could even see its heart beating.) There were colorful Amazon frogs and angelfish. In the corner of the store near the register, they had a thick-glassed aquarium with a real piranha. This was back before the fish was deemed contraband.

My father arrived early to the pet store carrying two large bags, so I had to stop browsing and shop in earnest. I bought

CHAPTER 32

ıs late when I climbed the porch to Mr.
er's house. After the last few days I
't know if he would even answer or, if
id, would let me in. I knocked on his
. His voice came weakly, "Come in."
ll shivering, I went inside, happy to be
of the cold and embraced by the warmth
s home.
. Foster was sitting in his chair near
fireplace. There was no music playing
the phonograph, and he didn't have a
. Beau was in his lap, and he was strok-
back his fur. It had been less than a
since I had last seen him, but, pecu-
, he didn't look the same. He looked
ıer in the face and shoulders, but his
ıach looked bigger. I shut the door
nd me.
'here is your coat?" he asked.
ran away."
looked sad. "Come sit by the fire." His

Beau a new leather collar with blue and red gems and a maroon wool dog coat. I thought Beau would really appreciate it on our walks since it had been so cold out.

The store even sold doggy shoes that fastened onto a dog's legs with drawstrings, but I figured that Beau was more likely to chew on them than to wear them. I thought they might be kind of embarrassing for him too, since no other dog was wearing them.

After the mall, my father and I drove over to the Iceberg, a drive-in just a mile from our home that was famous for thick milk-shakes and hamburgers. Unlike the mall, the drive-in wasn't crowded, probably since it was already past two and still snowing. Weather aside, this was turning out to be a pretty good day.

I ordered a cheeseburger, a bag of french fries, and a banana and caramel milk shake. My father and I sat down with our food near the back of the drive-in.

My father took a bite of his hamburger, then asked, "How much did you spend on your Christmas shopping?"

"That's private," I said.

"I'm sorry," he said. "Of course it is." We ate for a while in silence, then he said, "I bet you're going to be glad to get back to school next week."

I looked at him. "Why?"

"Routine is the bread of life."

"Moldy bread," I said.

He grinned. He took a sip of his drink, then said, "The hospital called this morning. They're releasing Mom tomorrow."

I wondered why he had waited until now to tell me. "What time?"

"They said I could pick her up anytime after one."

I was happy to hear this.

"I'm going to stay until Monday to make sure she's all right."

"You're leaving again?"

He was quiet for a moment, then said, "Son . . ." He breathed out slowly. "You should know I've come to a decision. I think it would be better all around if your mother and I got a divorce."

I stopped eating. Maybe breathing. My eyes welled up with tears. When I could speak, I asked, "Why do you hate us?"

"I don't hate you," he said.

I looked at him for a moment, then shouted, "Well, I hate you!" I sprang from my seat and ran out of the restaurant. My father shouted at me to come back, but I was gone. I just wished that I hadn't left my coat behind.

In running away I had cut through several

yards and found myself lost. Fo
half an hour I meandered throug
neighborhoods until, for the firs
I was glad to see Lincoln Ele
walked to my school. It was Sa
snowing, so the schoolyard was
Mrs. Covey's soul.

I walked over to the swing se
the snow off a plastic swing se
down. I began to swing back
Snow collected on me as tears
my cheeks.

The sky was already dark
cover, but now the sun had falle
horizon, leaving me alone in th
temperature fell with the sun,
hour I was shivering so hard th
chattered. I wished for the hun
that I had grabbed my coat. Stil
I'd rather freeze to death than b

Alone in the darkness and the
temperature, there was only
could think to go.

eyes looked heavy, the way my mother's looked during one of her migraines.

"Are you sick?" I asked.

"I don't sleep well these days," he said. "Have you heard from your mama?"

I sat down on the floor next to his chair. "My mother's coming home tomorrow."

"Praise God. I've been praying for her. And your papa."

Hearing the mention of my father made me angry. "My father says he wants a divorce." My eyes welled up. "Why does he hate us?"

Mr. Foster was silent for a moment, then said, "He doesn't hate you or your mama. He doesn't love himself. When people don't love themselves, they push the people they love away."

"Why doesn't he love himself?"

"Your father blames himself for your brother's death."

"No he doesn't."

Mr. Foster exhaled lightly. "I understand your papa better than you know." He paused for a moment, as if he was afraid to say what he wanted to say. When he spoke, his voice was strained. "I blamed myself for my son's death."

"You had a son who died?"

"My only son. Isaiah."

I didn't understand. "But you said he was alive."

"No. I never said that." He looked sadder than I had ever seen him. He looked up at the picture on the wall. "My son died a month after that photograph was taken."

I still didn't understand.

"My son died because of something I did." He pulled Beau in closer. "A long time ago I bought a refrigerator. Everyone has one these days, but back then, it was something special. Especially where we lived.

"When the men delivered it, the people in the neighborhood all came to see what I had bought. They stood in our front yard and watched them take it out of the truck. It was a celebration.

"A few weeks later Margaret and I were working out in the garden when Isaiah came out and said he was going to hide and asked me to come find him. I told him I would after we finished.

"When we went inside, I couldn't find my boy. I looked everywhere." His eyes moistened. "Then Margaret opened the refrigerator. Isaiah had climbed inside to hide from me. He had suffocated." Mr. Foster's chin began quivering. "I saw horrible things in the war. But there was nothing worse than seeing my own son in that refrigerator." A tear fell down his cheek.

When he could speak, he said, "Margaret was inconsolable. I knew she blamed me. I had bought the thing, and in her pain she needed someone to blame. When something that bad happens, sometimes we just need someone to put it on. Some people blame God. Margaret blamed me.

"I dragged that refrigerator out of the house and chopped a hole in it with an axe. Then, a week or so later, I moved out of the house to get away from my wife — just like your papa left your mama." He looked at me. "I should have stayed with her. She needed me, even if she didn't know it. But it was too painful. The truth was, I was too busy hating myself. Seeing my wife suffer only made it worse.

"Six months later Margaret was in a car accident. Some people said it wasn't an accident." He wiped his eyes. "I should have been there. But I was a coward. Shame can make cowards of us." He was silent for a moment, then looked back at me. "I was almost glad when the war started. I joined the very next day. I wasn't afraid to take a bullet. That's why I was upset the navy put me in a kitchen . . ." His words trailed off in silence.

"But you said you were going to visit them

for Christmas."

He nodded almost imperceptibly. "I've been making my way back to them for a long time now. Eight months ago, my liver stopped working. That's why my stomach looks like this. It keeps filling with fluid. Every week I go to the hospital to get it drained."

I was suddenly afraid. "How do they fix it?"

"Not everything in this life can be fixed," he said. He looked at me silently, then said, "I'm dying, Richard. My doctor didn't think I would live to Christmas."

His words froze my world.

When I could speak, I said, "No."

"I'm sorry."

My eyes welled up. "You can't leave, too."

He put his hand on my head. "I'm very sorry. You didn't need another loss in your life."

I closed my eyes tightly, pushing the tears out. Then I began to sob. For several minutes Mr. Foster just rubbed my head. Then he said, "I know it's hard, Richard. But if you can, we need to put that aside right now. I need to tell you something important about your papa."

I wiped my eyes, then looked up at him.

"You need to tell your papa that you know

it's not his fault that your brother died."

"He doesn't think it's his fault."

"He might not admit it, maybe not even to himself, but he does. More important, he needs to know that you *believe* it's not his fault. Believing is more powerful than knowing. Sometimes people know things that are true but don't believe them." He breathed out slowly. "He needs to believe that you still need him."

"It won't help," I said.

"Maybe it won't," he said softly. "But never underestimate how much we all need to be needed. Mr. Washington once said, 'Few things help someone more than to let them know that you believe in them.' "He looked me in the eyes. "You go tell him that. You let him know that you still believe in him."

"What if he still won't stay?"

Mr. Foster breathed out slowly. "He might not. That's the thing about people: as much as we wish we could control them, we can't. But at least you'll know that you tried. And someday that will bring you peace. Not right now, but someday."

I laid my head against his knee and cried. Mr. Foster just gently rubbed my hair. I didn't think my heart could take another good-bye.

CHAPTER 33

I was numb when I walked home. I didn't even notice the snow or cold. I opened the door of my house to find my father sitting in the front room, his fingers knit together. He was visibly upset. He stood when he saw me.

"Where have you been?"

"I went to Mr. Foster's house."

He breathed in deeply, calming himself, then he crossed the room to me. "Rick, I know this is hard. But you can't just run off like that. Something could have happened to you."

"I don't care what happens to me," I said. I rubbed my eyes. "Mr. Foster is dying."

My father's brows fell. "What?"

"Mr. Foster is going to die."

My father didn't know what to say. After a minute I wiped my eyes, then looked up at him. "I need to tell you something."

He gazed into my eyes.

"I know it's not your fault Mark died."

My father's expression immediately turned from soft to hard. "Why did you say that?"

"I wanted you to know."

His body tensed still more and his face turned red. "You think I don't know that? I know it's not my fault. It's the Pentagon's fault. It's those corrupt war-hawk politicians. It's the Viet Cong. They're the ones who took my son."

There was more silence. Then I said, "I miss Mark so much. I know you do, too. But I'm still here." I rubbed my nose. "I'm sorry I said I hate you. I don't. I need you. I need you to protect me. Me and Mom both do."

Tears welled up in my father's eyes. Then he said, "Protect you? Like I did your brother?" He turned and walked to his room.

I went to my bed and crawled under the blankets. I guessed that what Mr. Foster had told me to do was wrong after all.

Chapter 34

My mother came home Sunday afternoon. I hadn't seen my father all morning, though I could hear him busying about outside my bedroom. I wondered if he was already packing. Then, a little after noon, he left to get my mother. I just stayed in my room and read.

I came out of my room when I heard my father's car return. As I walked out there was a large bouquet of yellow daffodils on the table.

My mother and father were quiet as they walked into the house. My mother looked fragile, as if a puff of wind would blow her away. She walked straight to me and hugged me. "I'm so sorry, Ricky."

I shut my eyes tightly. I couldn't speak.

After a minute she said, "Whose are those?" I opened my eyes. She was looking at the flowers.

My father said, "I bought them for you."

Chapter 36

ked on the door, then walked in
Mr. Foster said anything. He was in
ne place he was the last time we'd
reclined on his armchair with Beau
p. He didn't look well.
ew you would come," he said.
't say anything. I held my lips tight.
that if I opened my mouth, sadness
vercome me.
mother told me that your father is

led.
ou tell him what I told you?"
ed again.
roud of you." Neither of us spoke
oment, then he looked at the bag I
ying. "What do you have there?"
d over and handed it to him, then
on the floor next to his armchair.
d inside the bag.
two presents on top are for

"They're beautiful. I love daffodils."

"I know," he said. Then, to my surprise, a tear fell down my father's cheek. It was the first time I'd seen him cry since my brother's funeral. For a moment we both watched him, unsure of what to say or do.

Then he said, "I'm sorry, June. I'm so, so sorry. I should have been there for Mark. I never should have let him go. I would trade places with him if I could."

A tear fell down my mother's cheek.

My father shook his head. "But I've only made things worse. I should have been there for you when you needed me. I let you down. I've let both of you down." He was silent for a moment, then said, "I don't know how to ask you to forgive me."

"You don't need our forgiveness," my mother said. "We have to own our choices. All of us. Mark too." She looked into his eyes. "I know you would have protected Mark if you could. What happened isn't your fault."

He lowered his head. "I don't believe that."

She stepped forward and took his head in her hands and lifted it to look into his eyes. "I do." For a moment they just looked into each other's eyes. Then they embraced. I walked over and joined them.

Chapter 35

My father stayed that night. He slept in the bedroom with my mother and never left. I was so grateful for that. I would have been happy, except there was something in my heart that kept me from it. It was something I was hiding from — as if denial would make it not so. I hadn't been back to see Mr. Foster since he told me he was dying.

Thursday, after school, I came home to find my mother waiting for me in the front room. From her demeanor I knew she had something important to say. I took off my coat, then sat down quietly across from her.

"Ricky, Mr. Foster called today . . . He would like to talk with you."

I didn't say anything.

"I think you should go talk to him."

I still didn't speak, but I could feel emotion rise in my chest.

"Ricky, he told me. I know that he's dying. I'm so sorry."

My eyes welled up.

"I know why you don't v
understand it's hard. Es
you've been through. H
believe how much you'v
You're the toughest kid
And, somehow, you still h
of anyone I've ever know
and kneeled next to me
been good to you. Wher
for you, he was. He's b
and that's a rare thing." S
"Right now, I think he ne
you be that for him?"

I looked down for nea
put my coat back on. I
gathered the Christmas
for him and Beau, then
Foster's house.

I knoc
before
the san
spoken,
in his la

"I kne

I didn
I knew
would c

"Your
home."

I nodd

"Did y

I nodd

"I'm p
for a mo
was carr

I walke
sat down
He looke

"The

Beau," I said.

He reached into the bag and brought out the first package. "Look at this," he said to Beau. "You've got Christmas." He carefully unwrapped the first gift. It was the collar.

"Look at those fancy gems on that, Beau." He held the collar in front of Beau. "You are going to be one fancy dog."

Beau just sniffed the collar.

"And you have another present, you lucky dog." He unwrapped the sweater, then held it out in front of Beau. "Isn't that something. You'll be the finest-dressed dog on the street."

"I didn't want him to be cold," I said.

"Just perfect for his long winter walks." He set the sweater down on top of the collar and looked at me. "Thank you, Richard."

"The other present is for you," I said.

He took the last gift from the bag and carefully unwrapped it. He lifted out the navy blue necktie. "Oh, my." He held the tie in front of him to admire it. "What a beautiful necktie." He looked at me. "I would like to wear this. Do you know how to tie it?"

I shook my head.

He just wrapped it around his neck. "This will have to do for now." He leaned over and hugged me. "Thank you."

"You're welcome."

"I have something for you, too, but first I need to talk to you about something very important."

"What do you want to talk about?" I asked.

"I want to talk to you about my death."

My eyes welled up. "I don't want to talk about that."

He exhaled deeply. "I don't want to, either. But sometimes the most important things to talk about are the things we don't want to." He looked at me for a long time. Then he said, "After I die, your heart will hurt like it did when your brother died. That's called grief. Has anyone ever talked to you about grief?"

I shook my head.

"Grief is a peculiar thing. It makes people act in funny ways. It makes them sad and angry and desperate. I've even seen it make people laugh at the most inappropriate time. It makes you feel like someone else has taken control of your heart. You can't help it. No one can. It's part of death.

"The world tries to pretend that death doesn't exist. It tries to hide it in whispers and back doors when really it's all around us — like the leaves falling in autumn.

"Grief is just opening our eyes to that

ıat Beau was going to be yours
·. I just had a sense about you. I
e first time we met that you and I
ng to be good friends for the rest of

I said.

l be my best friend for the rest of

d into the old man and he just held
 we could cry no more.

truth. We hate grief because it hurts. But not everything that hurts is bad. Whatever grief may be, it's one thing for certain. Grief is the truest evidence of love. And we should always be grateful to have something to love, even if it means that we have to lose it."

A tear fell down my cheek.

"That creek next to your house. It looks like it's always there, just as permanent as the trees on its bank. But it's not. It's never the same creek. Every day it's new water, and even though it looks the same, it never is. It's always flowing.

"That's the way life is. People will come and go your entire life. The best we can do is enjoy the water while it's there."

He put his hand under Beau's chin and slightly lifted it. "Think of our Beau here. A little dog like him won't live more than fifteen years. That means that someday we'll have to say good-bye to him. What an awful day that will be. But would it be better if we never knew him?"

I didn't answer.

"Richard, would it?"

I shook my head. "No."

"No. Think of all the love we'd miss out on." He scratched Beau under his chin. "It's a peculiar thing, but oftentimes it's the brevity of a thing that makes something valuable. A sunset fills our souls, not just because it's beautiful, but because it's fleeting." He looked at the Christmas tree. "And Christmas wouldn't be special if it was here all the time, would it?"

Tears fell down my cheeks. "I'm tired of losing things."

"I know," he said softly. "I know." He took a deep breath. "You once said to me that nothing lasts. In a way, you were right. But there's something ironic about that. Do you know what *ironic* means?"

I shook my head.

"Ironic is when something turns out to be very different than what we think it should be. You said that nothing lasts, but if that's true, it means that death doesn't last, either. You're right about that. Because, in the end, even that old creek ends up somewhere. And that is hopeful. Because it means that somewhere, there is a place where nothing ends.

"I suppose that's why I'm not afraid to die. That's what Christmas is about. It's about celebrating things that live past this life. Jesus was born so we can live forever.

"And that means I'll see my son and wife again. It means I'll see you and Beau again. And it means you'll see your brother again." He looked me closely in the eyes. "There is

a place where nothing ends
that?"

I was still for a moment,

He exhaled deeply. "I
there's one more thing. I
favor of you. May I do tha

"Yes."

"After I'm gone, there w
take care of Beau. Would
him for me?"

"You want me to take B

"Yes. I've already asked
said it would be all righ
down at the little dog, hi
welling with tears. "He'
present, now. You could t
you want."

I looked at Beau, then l
"He needs to stay with
stopped.

He slightly smiled, the
dog's head. "I love this li
it was Beau who brough
a smart dog."

"Gollum," I said. "He'

Mr. Foster looked at m
edly, laughed. "Gollur
name for such a sweet d
at me fondly. "You know
I knew the first time I s

fenc
some
knew
were
my li
"N
"N
"Yo
mine.
I le
me u

Epilogue

Mr. Foster left us on Christmas Day. It was one of the hardest days of my life. Still, a part of me was happy that he got to spend Christmas as he hoped — with his wife and son. He was buried wearing his new necktie. He finally had a reason to wear one.

The last thing I said to Mr. Foster was true. I have cherished and held his friendship in my heart my entire life.

The young Black woman I saw visiting Mr. Foster's house was a lawyer who had come to help him make his final will. Since he had no living family, Mr. Foster had his house put in a trust and sold. Half the money went to the United Negro College Fund. The other half went to my college fund. All his savings went into a special account for me as well. He really did treat me as a son.

Mr. Foster also left me his Japanese Kintsugi vase. I'm told it's worth a lot of money, but that doesn't matter to me. Nothing could make me sell it. Its personal value is far greater to me than the gold that holds it together.

The principle the vase represents is true. The broken parts of our lives can not only be made whole again, they can be made stronger. My family never separated again. All families suffer, and all have scars, but, like the vase, those broken places can be stronger and gilded and more beautiful when healed.

Our family was blessed with many years together. My mother died of breast cancer on Valentine's Day in 2009. She was seventy-two years old. My father had left a single red rose and a card on the nightstand next to her bed before going out to make her breakfast. As far as we know, she never read it. When he came back, she was gone.

I read the card. It said,

> June, wherever you are, wherever you go, I love you and I always will.

The spray on my mother's casket was made of daffodils. It wasn't until then that I learned the significance of the daffodils my father had left on the table the day he came back. Daffodils were special to my mother.

She said they were the first flowers to lift their heads after a hard winter, and a reminder that after every winter there comes spring. If we can just hold on through the cold.

My father was never the same after my mother died. He passed away just two years later of natural causes. He was seventy-nine.

My dear friend Beau is gone. I miss that sweet little dog. It wasn't until my late teens that I understood that Mr. Foster didn't give me Beau so I could watch over him. He gave me Beau to watch over me. I like to think of the great reunion he and Mr. Foster must have had. I'm sure Beau has licked his face a million times since then.

Life goes on. As my brother and Mr. Foster conspired, I discovered the power of books. One day I took the leap from reading them to writing them. I'm certain that they would approve of my chosen profession. There are times that thoughts and passages come to me and I wonder if, perhaps, Mark and Booker are my muses, imparting their wisdom to me, just as they did in life.

I have penned dozens of books and traveled around the world to meet my readers. Through it all, I have learned that we are all much more alike than we ever imagined, and that our most secret thoughts are often the most universal. This is hopeful to me. We are not as far apart as we sometimes believe.

Today, I am nearly the same age Mr. Foster was when we first met. I have my own family; my wife, four daughters, and a son. My children are grown now. I have two beautiful grandchildren. The cycle begins anew.

Day by day, my life continues down that old creek, as all our lives must. Time has taught me that I am not just a spectator on that creek, but that I am the water, moving steadily along to a place where nothing ends.

I've learned that along that creek's banks there are occasional Christmas trees, bedecked and bright, marking our passage along the flow of time. These are among my favorite memories and now and then, I take them out, like old photographs from a shoebox, to warm my heart on cold days. I cherish all my Christmas memories, but perhaps none so much as that Christmas with Mr. Foster and Beau.

Someday, in the not-so-distant future, I too will go, leaving behind my loved ones and a book or two. In the end, our lives are short, which is all the more reason to greet each day with joy and love and purpose. As Mr. Foster said, oftentimes it's the brevity

of a thing that makes it most

There are so many profou
Foster said to me, but perha
than this: "Grief is the true
love. And we should always
have something to love even
we have to lose it." I know t
in the moment of loss, ho
sweet blade cuts.

And perhaps that is why v
mases, to remind us over an
the end, there is a place v
broken will be made whole
lost will be found — that t
where love doesn't end. An
remind us that, in the end, l

ACKNOWLEDGMENTS

I'm very grateful to Jennifer Bergstrom; Jennifer Long; Aimée Bell; my agent, Laurie Liss; and my editor, Hannah Braaten, for not only going along with my desire to share this unique story but the passion you brought to the project. I'm so grateful that I get to work with you all. Aimée, your experience reading my manuscript made me smile for many days.

I'm grateful to my assistant, Diane Glad, for fourteen years of help and encouragement. Also to her husband, Robert, who patiently puts up with it all.

This book was difficult for my wife, Keri, to read, since she alone knows how much of it is true. I'm grateful to have had her at my side on my ride down that creek.

A GIFT FOR MY READERS

Many have asked for the coveted recipes shared in this book — particularly my grandmother's Parker House Rolls recipe and Mr. Foster's Thumbprint Cookie recipe. If you would like these recipes, just go to richardpaulevans.com and click on the "A Christmas Memory Recipes" button. We will email them to you, along with a special gift. Blessings!

ABOUT THE AUTHOR

Richard Paul Evans is the #1 *New York Times* and *USA TODAY* bestselling author of more than forty novels. There are currently more than thirty-five million copies of his books in print worldwide, translated into more than twenty-four languages. Richard is the recipient of numerous awards, including two first place Storytelling World Awards, the *Romantic Times* Best Women's Novel of the Year Award, and is a five-time recipient of the Religion Communicators Council's Wilbur Awards. Seven of Richard's books have been produced as television movies. His first feature film, *The Noel Diary,* starring Justin Hartley (*This Is Us*) and acclaimed film director, Charles Shyer (*Private Benjamin, Father of the Bride*), will debut in 2022. In 2011 Richard began writing Michael Vey, a #1 New York Times bestselling young adult series which has won more than a dozen awards. Richard is the founder of The Christmas Box International, an organization devoted to maintaining emergency children's shelters and providing services and resources for abused, neglected, or homeless children and young adults. To date, more than 125,000 youths have been helped by the charity. For his humanitarian work, Richard has received the *Washington Times* Humanitarian of the Century Award and the Volunteers of America National Empathy Award. Richard lives in Salt Lake City, Utah, with his wife, Keri, and their five children and two grandchildren. You can learn more about Richard on his website richardpaulevans.com.

The employees of Thorndike Press hope you have enjoyed this Large Print book. All our Thorndike, Wheeler, and Kennebec Large Print titles are designed for easy reading, and all our books are made to last. Other Thorndike Press Large Print books are available at your library, through selected bookstores, or directly from us.

For information about titles, please call:
(800) 223-1244

or visit our website at:
gale.com/thorndike

To share your comments, please write:
Publisher
Thorndike Press
10 Water St., Suite 310
Waterville, ME 04901